THE MARRIAGE ARRANGEMENT

ANYTHING FOR LOVE

KIM LORAINE

Copyright © 2022 by Kim Loraine

All rights reserved.

No part of this book may be reproduced in any form or by any electronic or mechanical means, including information storage and retrieval systems, without written permission from the author, except for the use of brief quotations in a book review.

Editor: Comma Sutra Editorial Services

Photography: Wander Aguiar

Cover Design: T.E. Black Designs

THE MARRIAGE ARRANGEMENT

USA TODAY BESTSELLING AUTHOR
KIM LORAINE

1

SAVAGE

I stood outside Becca's house, my stomach churning with the knowledge of what I was about to do. I'd been awake for hours, gone for a punishing run, showered, dressed, and hopped on a ferry before the sun was even up. Now the manila envelope in my hand felt like it was a fucking explosive as I held it and waited for this fiery little blonde baker to open the door.

Hopefully I'd caught her before she and Scarlett began baking for the day. She'd said things got going early, but I hadn't thought to ask exactly *how* early. By the scent of melted butter and sugar filling the air, I was clearly too late.

I rang the doorbell, hoping she'd answer and I wouldn't have to deal with her wide-eyed sister. But no one came to the door.

"Bloody fucking hell," I muttered as I adjusted my cap and zipped my jacket to my chin. It was baltic this morning without my cold weather running gear on.

I banged on the door, calling out, "Becca, let me in, lass. I'm freezing my bollocks off out here."

Something hit me in the back of the head, making me spin around to find the culprit. There she was, the one who got away. More like the one who never gave me a fair shake at winning her.

Becca Barnes stood behind me with a yellow apron tied around her front, her hair in a bun atop her head, and flour streaking one cheek. She also had a wad of dough in her tiny wee fist.

"Did you just assault me with . . . cookie dough, lass?"

"Yeah, I did. What are you going to do about it, Taylor?"

"That's a real waste. I thought you were meant to be a baker. Bakers . . . bake, don't they?"

She cocked her hip and lifted her chin defiantly. "Normally, yes, we do. This morning is an exception. What are you doing here?"

"I needed to see you."

"Why? We've said everything we need to say."

"No, we haven't."

"You could have texted me."

"Aye, but then you'd have been able to ignore me."

Her gaze traveled my body until she stopped

on the envelope in my hands. "Oh God. Are you suing me for some bullshit reason? Taylor, I can't afford to be sued. I'm barely keeping things going as it is."

"No, I'm not suing you. Why would I be suing you?"

Her shoulders loosened and she looked relieved. "Then why are you here?"

"Can we go inside? I'm fucking frozen."

She rewarded me with an expression that said I was full of shit. "You're a hockey player. It's thirty-five degrees out here. Don't you have, like, superhuman powers of cold deflection?"

"While I love that you think I'm a superhero—"

"Villain."

"I'm not dressed like a hockey player. I still get cold. Besides, if memory serves, you like a bad boy."

Her cheeks went pink, and she huffed out a breath. I could see it in the air, a little puff of annoyance at herself for her reaction to me. This could work. This might be the in I needed.

"Let me in, lass. I need to ask you something."

She sighed. "Fine. I was about to take a coffee break anyway. Follow me."

We walked around the little house until we reached a converted garage, complete with a bakery truck with a logo splashed across the side that read *BSB Bakery*. The delicious scent of baked goods was stronger over here, and my stomach growled.

"How do you stand it?"

"Stand what?"

"Working in these conditions? I'd eat it all and never sell a single thing."

She shrugged. "I like money."

"Fair."

Music blared from inside the garage-turned-kitchen, and I caught sight of Scarlett working with a piping bag, her brow furrowed in concentration as she decorated a three-tiered cake.

"This is where you bake everything? And you sell out of that little truck?" I asked, disbelief coloring my words.

"For now, yeah. We're leasing a space downtown, but our entire kitchen needs to be gutted and redone."

"Sounds expensive."

She took a tight breath, that tension returning to her shoulders and around her eyes. "It is." Then she leaned in through the doorway and called, "Scar! I'm taking a coffee break."

Her sister looked up from what she was doing long enough to give me a double take and then offered a thumbs up before going back to work.

"Come on. Coffee's in the house."

We went inside through a door around back and came right into the cozy kitchen. Immediate warmth hit me. "Thank fuck. Heat."

"You're a wuss."

"You're clearly a yeti. You're not even wearing a coat."

She shrugged, then headed for the coffeepot on the counter, blessedly full, and grabbed two mugs. "Cream? Sugar?"

"Just a bit of cream."

After getting us our coffees, she motioned to the kitchen table, and we sat facing each other.

"So what in the world brings the bad boy of Seattle hockey to my doorstep at seven in the morning?"

"I need you to marry me."

She choked on her coffee, spitting it all over the table. "I'm sorry, say that again?"

"You heard me. I need you to marry me. Today."

"Why would I do that? I don't even like you."

That stung, but I'd earned it. "Oh, come on, Tink. You like me at least a little. You've let me put my tongue—"

"Stop right there. That was a mistake I made. I might like your tongue, but the man attached to it leaves a lot to be desired."

"What if I offered to pay for your new kitchen in exchange for your hand in marriage?"

"What is this, the Middle Ages? No."

"Just in name. We don't have to . . . you know."

"No, Taylor, I don't know. What in God's

name could be so bad that you'd need a wife to get out of it?"

This was it. The moment of truth. I took a deep breath and raked a hand through my hair as I pulled together the words I wanted to say.

"Look, this app thing is getting out of control. They want me to be on some reality show next and sign a five-year endorsement deal."

"Isn't that just money in your pocket?"

"No. I mean . . . it is, but it's also me being forced to use this bonkers app, date women I don't really like, then post about it, and, you know, sell my soul for profit."

"Aw, you poor baby. You're famous and being used by the big bad corporations for their financial gain. Must be hard."

"I'm serious, Becca. I'll pay for a state-of-the-art kitchen. I'll take care of you."

She sat back and crossed her arms over her chest. "I don't need you to take care of me."

"I know that. I just . . . I need help, and this is the only way I can get out of this bloody contract."

"How long?"

"What?"

"How long do we have to be married?"

"A year, just to be safe."

Her brows shot into her hairline. "An entire *year*? Are you crazy?"

"And we have to live together."

"*What?* You said in name only. I can't move off the island. I need to be close to the bakery. To Scarlett."

I'd already thought of this. I'd thought of everything. "I'll buy a house nearby. We can live there."

"Why do we have to live together?"

"The contract with *Meet-Cupid* stipulates the agreement is void if I'm married and in a committed, co-habitant relationship."

She bit her lower lip and trained her gaze on the coffee mug in front of her. "You'll redo the kitchen exactly how we want it? No questions asked?"

"Aye."

"I get my own room?"

"Aye." My chest tightened in anticipation as she was obviously warming to the idea.

"One year living with you. Do I have to pretend to love you?"

"Only when we attend public functions. And we'll need to post on social media every now and then."

"But other than that, I can go about my life?"

"With the exception of dating. I can't have my wife dating other men."

"And you won't see other women." She said it like a statement, not a question.

"Aye, you'll be my moon and stars, lass."

"I don't see how we're going to do this today. We need a license, an officiant."

I placed the envelope on the table. "Taken care of."

She opened the flap and pulled out the marriage license I'd applied for, both of our names already written down. "Are you serious? You knew I'd say yes?"

"I hoped so. You're a smart woman, business-minded, and even though you say you hate me, you don't really."

"I do."

"Look, you already know your lines."

She rolled her eyes. "Not helping your case, Taylor."

"Fine, hate me. But I need you to marry me tonight before the auction, love me or hate me."

"I suppose you've already booked an appointment at city hall too?"

I smirked. "Aye. And I've got a suit in my car."

She took a heavy breath, then let it out in a rush. "What time is the appointment?"

2

THREE MONTHS EARLIER

BECCA

"A dating app wants to sponsor the team?" I asked my sister Clara as we sat together in the living room of the house they'd just moved into.

I bounced my baby niece Quinn in my lap, her little gurgles of pleasure making me smile through the stress of the last few weeks.

"Yeah, they got a look at the roster and think it's a perfect match. Hot hockey boys. What's not to love?"

"Hot, huh? You been lookin' Mrs. Wilde?" My brother-in-law, Maverick, sauntered in from the kitchen, a tool belt around his waist and a smirk on his lips.

"You know I have a thing for cowboys, Mav. Not puck boys." Clara's cheeks went pink.

He leaned down and kissed her before plucking Quinn off my lap and giving her loud kisses on her neck until she giggled.

"That's right, mama only likes cowboys." He snuggled her close. "Tell your mama her sink is all fixed and she should come give her favorite cowboy some sugar."

Clara gave him a smile so full of adoration my stomach twisted as she stood and laid a kiss on him. I rolled my eyes. They were so in love it hurt to look at them.

"Well, you can count me out when it comes to this dating app. I'm not interested. Is it too much to ask for to just meet someone the old-fashioned way?"

Mav cocked one brow. "I happen to love doing things the old-fashioned way, Becs. I think more people should try it."

Clara smirked. "Of course you do."

"Yes, we all know. Now please never remind me how you and Clara..."

"That's enough. Aren't you supposed to meet Scarlett at the bakery location? You need to get out of here before you're late. She'll freak."

I glanced at my phone and saw I had missed two texts from our sister.

"Well, shit. I'll never make it to the space in time. She moved up the walk-through."

"Who did?"

"The landlord. I swear, she doesn't want us to rent the space."

Mav jerked his chin toward the door. "Come on, I'll take you to the ferry. You'll make it in time. Just have a little faith."

Scarlett was too sweet. It made her a pushover, easy to take advantage of. This was a prime example. We weren't supposed to meet for the walk-through until this afternoon. Which meant I should have had plenty of time for this visit and to get home for lunch before we had this meeting. Now everything was shot to hell.

I stared down at the texts on my phone.

Scarlett: Can you be here now? She wants to get this done so she can get an earlier flight for her vacation.

Scarlett: Where are you? I told her we could make it.

Scarlett: I don't want to go alone. I'm not as good at negotiating as you.

"Shit," I muttered as I hitched my bag over my shoulder.

Me: Don't sign anything until I'm there.

Of course, even with Mav tearing through the Seattle streets, I didn't make the ferry. I waited in the terminal, legs bouncing with anxiety, hoping for a response from Scar.

The walk-on crowd began loading onto the boat, people chatting happily, quite a few couples holding hands, carrying fresh bouquets from Pike Place Market.

I sighed, letting nostalgia wash over me for the barest second. I'd had that once upon a time. True love, or so I'd thought. Until he got drafted by the NFL and left his college girlfriend behind. Hint . . . I was the college girlfriend. I'd been so young and wide-eyed. Now I just laugh at the girl I used to be. The one who believed in fate and love, romance and the 'good ones.' Now I know they don't exist. No matter how much we want them to.

I sat quietly, scrolling through Scar's social media posts for the bakery, responding to emails and comments, until the ferry docked and I could finally run for the storefront location.

Sun beamed through the window as I sat on one of the bench seats, the vinyl creaking with every shift of my hips. It was a full boat today, the weekend crowd getting out of the city and heading for the charm of the island.

My phone buzzed in my hand, a message from Scar.

Scarlett: I signed the lease. As is. I'm sorry, she wouldn't wait.

"What? No! Oh, shit on a shingle."

A low chuckle from behind me had me turning around to face a tall tattooed man sitting in the booth behind me. He was manspread across the entirety of the bench, his dark ball cap pulled down over his eyes.

"Something funny?"

Tilting his head up, he flashed me a panty-melting grin.

"Aye, lass. You."

"You're laughing at me?"

The man raised his face, hitting me with a mischievous grin. "Your nose does this adorable crinkly thing when you're cross. With your blonde hair and that green shirt, you look a wee bit like Tinkerbell."

The only thing that kept me talking to him was the Scots accent. I swear. That was it—except for the tattoos running down his forearms and peeking out above the collar of his henley. Okay, so there was more than just the accent.

I couldn't tell if he was flirting or just a friendly, playful person. "Does that make you Peter Pan?"

"Oh, no, my wee darlin'. That makes me Captain Hook. I'm too much of a bad boy to be claiming anything more gallant."

"You know Captain Hook poisoned Tinkerbell, right?"

"No. He tried to poison Peter Pan. Tink got in the middle. She saved him."

"Same difference." I shrugged.

"Ah, but that's where you're wrong. What if

Hook was the one Tink should've been pining for all along? Peter was a spoiled brat who didn't know what he had. Hook saw right through him. She should've allied herself with the pirates. She would've been better off."

My lips twitched in a smile. I couldn't stop myself. "Okay. You keep telling yourself that. Clearly you've got an untapped villain arc you need to explore."

Turning away from him, I stared out the window as the boat sailed toward Bainbridge. We were very nearly there already, the crossing only taking thirty minutes. Soon I'd be on my way to the house I shared with Scarlett, hopeful she hadn't made a decision that would bankrupt our fledgling bakery. The hot Scot plopped down in the bench seat across from me, invading my space with his cocky smirk. "So you don't like a bad boy, then, lass?"

I shook my head and forced my gaze everywhere but on him. "No. It's been my experience that all bad boys stay bad. Even when they pretend they're reformed."

"Have a lot of experience with that?"

"Once is enough."

His face turned serious. "I'm sorry to hear that."

"I'm sorry I have to say it." The boat slowed as one of the crew came over the intercom and announced our arrival. As the crowd of walk-on passengers lined up, ready to disembark, I typed a quick message to Scarlett and slowly gathered my things.

"Aren't you coming?"

"Sure. But I'll wait for the boat to actually dock. I don't need to wait in this line when there's a perfectly good seat right here. My car will still be parked in the lot when I get off."

"You live over here?"

"I do. Why? Are you planning to stalk me? I'm really not that interesting."

"Oh, I beg to differ. You're the most interesting woman I've met since I got here."

As the crowd began moving and people exited the ferry, the Scot waited for me, gaze expectant. "Why are you looking at me like you're a lost puppy?"

"No reason. I just thought perhaps you'd like to walk with me? I don't want to leave you alone on your way to your car. What if something should happen?"

"It's the middle of the day."

"Anything can happen any time of day, Tink."

"Is that a threat?"

"What? No. Of course not. What are you trying to say? Do I look like the kind of wanker who preys on innocent pixies?"

"I am not a pixie."

"I think ye are."

"And you're an arrogant oaf."

He snorted. "That's the truth. I like you, Tinkerbell. Now, come on, the boat is nearly empty. Don't they kick you off anyway? There's no avoiding this. We're walking together. But if it makes you feel better, I won't watch you go to your car, all right?"

I sighed. "Fine."

"Which one's that fine for?"

"All of it?"

"Are you sure?"

"Yes. We can part ways at the terminal."

"I'll take it. I'm Taylor, by the way."

"Becca. It's nice to meet you."

The way his blue eyes flashed and a smirk tipped up his lips had my heart fluttering in a way it hadn't in a long time. Oh, he knew exactly what he was doing. His palm rested on my lower back as we joined the line of people leaving, the two of us taking up the rear and walking slowly. "Would you believe me if I said this was the first time I've been over this way?"

"Actually, yes, that tracks."

"So, do you have any tips for a tourist? What should I make sure to see?"

"Well, there are lots of little places downtown. Wineries, restaurants, galleries. And I'm really partial to the Japanese garden."

We reached the terminal, but he didn't take his hand off the small of my back, and I didn't want him to. I liked the feel of him touching me. I liked how he smelled, crisp and fresh, like clean laundry and mint.

"Would you like to show me around the town, Tink? Maybe we could go to the gardens you mentioned?" His voice was filled with nervous energy, sweet and hopeful. My shoulders sagged as I glanced toward the sliding doors which led out to the parking lot. Part of me wanted to say yes, but the other, bigger part said, you have so much on your plate right now. A fling with a hot Scot isn't on the menu.

I licked my lips, turning to face him. He towered over me, the tension between us pulling me toward him rather than pushing me away. "Come on, lass. What do you say? Be a little bad with me?"

"I..."

"Would the passenger who belongs to an orange Jeep Wrangler please return to your vehicle and disembark the vessel?" blared over the loudspeaker.

"Bloody hell."

I couldn't keep from laughing. "Wait. You drove on the ferry?"

"I might've done."

"What are you waiting for? Go. They can't load the boat if you don't leave. They'll tow you."

He pulled his phone from his pocket and looked at me expectantly.

"What are you doing?"

"I'm programming your number into my phone. What does it look like I'm doing?"

I couldn't stop grinning. "Oh, is that what's happening here?"

"Aye. Don't be the reason my car gets towed off the boat, Tink."

I rolled my eyes. "Fine."

Then I rattled off my digits for him.

"Would the passenger with the ostentatious orange Jeep Wrangler please return to your vehicle aboard ship and disembark the vessel?"

I slapped him lightly on the shoulder. "Go. You have my number. You can find me. Get out of here."

He winked. "I'll be in touch, Tink. You can count on it."

Then he turned and jogged back toward the boat. I wasn't ashamed to say I watched his ass the whole way. My smile didn't falter as I walked to my car or even as I got in. And then, when my phone buzzed in my purse and I looked at the screen, that smile turned to a laugh accompanied by a racing heart.

Unknown: I told you I'd be in touch, lass. If you change your mind and decide you want to spend some time with a bad influence, give me a call. Taylor.

3

TAYLOR

I knew it was her the moment I saw the fall of her blond locks as I walked into my favorite coffee shop in Seattle. Becca sat in a cozy chair nestled into the corner of the room, A tablet open, and a frown of concentration on her face. I didn't think twice about going to talk to her. It'd been a week since I saw her last. I needed a fix.

"So it seems we meet again, this time on my side of the water," I said, approaching Becca.

She smiled, her eyes bright and amused as I took a seat across from her.

"Taylor, right?"

"Aye, lass, and you are Becca."

"That's right. Good memory."

"Of course I remember you. There's no way I could forget you, my little Tinkerbell."

"I don't know why you insist on calling me that. I am not a pixie at five foot six."

"Well, you're tiny to me." Her cheeks flamed pink. "And there's just something about you. Maybe it's the blonde locks or the attitude." I shrugged. "You're pixie-like."

"I guess we'll have to agree to disagree on that."

"Maybe. So what are you doing over here?"

"I had a meeting with a potential client, but they no-showed me."

"In that case, do you mind if I join you?"

Her sweet smile had me relaxing instantly. "Well, it looks like you already have."

She motioned to where I was sitting.

"If you don't want company, I can find somewhere else."

"No, it's nice to see a friendly face. Don't you work, though? It's the middle of the day during the week."

And here it was, the moment it was all out there. "My . . . schedule is a little more relaxed."

"What does that mean? Are you a paperboy or something? Do you only work at night?"

"No, I'm not a paperboy."

Before I could tell her what I did, a pair of young women pointed and giggled as they realized who I was. Bugger, I shouldn't have taken off my bloody hat. The closer they got, the younger they appeared. And finally, they approached me.

"Can we get a picture?" one asked, her eyes shining.

"Of course." They flanked me, and I held out each of their phones one after the other and took a photo. "Have a nice day, lassies."

They giggled at my Scottish accent. To be fair, I was laying it on pretty thick for them. They ran off without so much as a request for a hug and—thank God—no slyly delivered phone numbers.

Becca narrowed her eyes at me. "What was that?"

"My job."

"Your job is to take photos with girls young enough to land you in jail?"

Fuck. No. This wasn't going well at all. "I'm a professional hockey player, and sometimes I get recognized. Fans want to take photos and have me sign things."

"Oh my God. You play for the Cyclones."

And here it was, that awkward moment it dawned on her. She was a fan, and she hadn't realized she was talking to me.

"Aye. I do."

"Taylor Savage."

"Yes."

"Taylor Savage. The Scottish one. How did I not see it before?"

"Maybe you weren't looking hard enough."

"Maybe."

"Are you a hockey fan?"

She shrugged. "No, not really. I only watch because my sister makes me."

"Your sister makes you watch hockey?"

Now it was her turn to look embarrassed. "Her husband is Maverick Wilde."

All the air punched from my lungs. "Your sister is Clara Wilde? She owns the Cyclones."

"Technically her husband owns them."

"If she's married to him, she owns them too."

"What are the chances?"

"Right, I suppose you could say that." Bloody hell, this thing between us just went from easy to fucking complicated.

"Anyway, now I understand why you looked a little familiar. I've watched you slam people up against the boards pretty regularly, although everyone just calls you Savage."

"They do."

"But you didn't want me to know. Why not?"

"Let's just say I like the sound of my first name on your lips."

"Oh, you are smooth, Mr. Savage."

"And you are dead sexy, Miss . . ."

"Barnes."

The barista announced my order was up, and I headed toward the pickup counter, wishing I didn't have to leave Becca for even a moment. I didn't care that she was the team owner's sister-in-law. I just wanted to be around her. I never said I was a smart man.

As I returned with a warm pastry and a cup of steaming hot coffee, I couldn't help but gaze at her and wonder what those lips would taste like. Especially when she took a sip from her own mug and then ran her tongue across her bottom lip to capture one last drop. God, I was jealous of her drink.

"That looks good," she said, gesturing to my pastry.

"Aye, fresh berry tart. Did you want a bite?"

"You would share with me?"

"Of course I would."

"That's sweet." Her cheeks went pink.

"So are you." I sat across from her, placing the plate between us. "Now tell me about this client you were supposed to meet with. What do you do?"

"I have a bakery, and I was meeting a potential client."

"Was?"

"Yeah, apparently they just called off their wedding, so my services are no longer required."

The way her nose scrunched as she said the last words made my lips quirk into a smile. "Oh, that doesn't sound good."

"It's not. Kind of a high-profile wedding. It would've been big for me. But, further proof true love isn't real, and people shouldn't waste their time trying to find it. Those two were doomed from the start." She leaned in conspiratorially. "But don't tell anyone I said that. Bad for business."

I mimed zipping my lips. "You'll no hear a word from my lips about it."

"Good."

"You really don't believe in love?"

She shook her head.

"Why?"

"My parents got married for all the wrong reasons."

"Aye, so did mine. It's a hazard."

"Mine stayed married for all the wrong reasons. They died trying to fix a marriage that wasn't real."

That little nugget of information had my heart dropping to my stomach, a cold pit forming.

"Are you serious, Tink?"

"It was a car accident. They were on their way to a marriage retreat." The way she had to swallow back tears gutted me. "I was really little. I don't remember that well. My sister basically raised my younger sister and me."

"Clara did?"

"Yeah, she's pretty amazing."

I thought of the strong-willed veterinarian whose husband had inherited my team. Clara

Wilde was amazing, and so was her sister. "I do like her quite a bit. She's a good woman."

"She is one of the best. I'm glad she comes up here so often now. I wish they would move here."

"You never know. Maybe she will. It's hard not to fall in love with Seattle."

That smile was back in her eyes as she let my words sink in. "Enough about me. Tell me about you, Taylor Savage. A hockey player from Scotland . . . I thought rugby would be more your style."

"Why? Because I'm braw and rugged?"

Her laugh filled the room. "Because the only guy I knew from Scotland played rugby."

"Ah, so it's a stereotype, is it? I see. Would you like to ask me what's under my kilt now too?"

Pink darkened her cheeks. "You're not wearing a kilt."

I couldn't help myself. I leaned in and gave her a wink. "No, I'm not, but I can guarantee you, I'm wearing the same thing under my joggers as I would under a kilt."

"That's . . . a lot of information."

"About my underpants? Aye, it is. You brought it up. You're a naughty little pixie, aren't you?" I was pushing my luck, but she was so easy to rile up. "I'm only teasing you, lass. I like to go fast. I'm faster on the ice than I am on the ground. Simple as that."

"That sounds exhilarating." Her eyes brightened. "I've never been on the ice before in my life."

"Are you serious? I can't believe no one's taken you out."

She shrugged. "There hasn't really been an opportunity."

"Well, what are you doing right now?"

"Not a thing. I blocked off my whole day for this client who stood me up."

Excitement built in my belly. I drained my drink, then snagged Becca's cup before taking the rubbish to the bin. By the time I returned, Becca had closed her laptop and put it away. She stared at me curiously.

"What was that?"

"Just trying to make sure everything's ready."

"Ready for what?"

"Our date."

"Date? I don't remember you asking me on a date."

"Consider this me asking. Neither of us has anything till tomorrow anyway. You're all mine . . . hopefully." Why did I have butterflies in my stomach?

"That's ambitious."

"Well, I like to know what's possible before getting into anything."

"And you think I'm going to sleep with you?"

"I didn't say that."

"No, but you implied it."

Holding out a hand, I waited for her to make her choice. "You never know. You might be so tired out you have to spend the night on my couch."

"Sure." She gave me a knowing grin and fitted her palm into mine. "So you're taking me skating?"

"You'd like to go, wouldn't you?"

"Yes, I would. But I'm going to fall on my ass."

"Of course you are. That's part of skating. I still fall on my arse sometimes."

Her brows lifted. "Do you? Are you teasing me?"

"I was humoring you. There's a difference."

"Okay, Taylor. One date. But I'm not sleeping with you."

All I needed was one date. One night with her to make her see we'd be good together. This was my shot. I had to take it.

Twenty minutes later, we were at a local ice rink where I regularly volunteered to coach a youth league, along with a few of my teammates.

"Hi, Savage." Jeanette, a woman in her forties who ran the office, greeted me as soon as I walked through the doors. "Frank didn't tell me you were gonna be here. The boys coming too?"

"No, just me and Becca here. Can you get her some skates?" I hefted my bag over my shoulder, still containing my practice gear and hockey skates.

Jeanette slid her gaze to Becca. "Size?"

"Eight," Becca said, her hand gripping mine.

"Of course. Give me just a minute."

"Get her some good ones," I called. "Not any of those dull blades."

Jeanette came back with a pair and handed them to me.

"Thank you, darling. You're a star." I winked at her.

"Public session starts in ten minutes. You two can go ahead and get out there."

Becca and I walked to a bench, and I hated that I had to take my palm off the small of her back so we could get our skates on.

"How long have you been doing this?" she asked, watching me pull my trainers off.

"Since I was two or so. It was the one thing I was good at."

We sat on the benches, and I laced my skates as she tugged off her shoes. She was so bonnie I didn't even look at my feet while I tied my laces. I just stared at her face as she worked the skates on. Her brows furrowed as she pulled on the laces, little grunts of concentration escaping. Fuck. What would she look like concentrating on coming with my tongue on her clit?

"Taylor?" Her voice broke through my salacious inspection of the skates.

"What was that?"

"I asked if I got these tight enough."

My God, I was a mess. If she glanced at my crotch, she'd know I wasn't checking out the boots. I was fantasizing about taking them off her and throwing her onto my bed.

"You really throw yourself around a sheet of ice all day?"

"That's right. And some people say I'm pretty good at it." Reaching out, I gave her laces a tug, tightening them on each skate before nodding and saying, "All right, I think we're good to go here. Are you ready?"

"As I'll ever be."

I took her hand, and we walked through the double doors separating the rink from the lobby. A shiver had her nestling a little deeper into my borrowed hoodie. "You weren't kidding. It's freezing."

"You've been inside an ice rink before."

"Yeah, one time in the owner's box. Nice and warm. No risk of falling."

"I can't believe I haven't seen you before. You were right there, under my nose."

I threaded our fingers, my chest tightening at the sensation racing through me just from touching her. God, I'd never survive her.

"Come on, lass. I swear to you, I willnae let you fall."

I stepped out onto the ice and waited for her.

"Promise?"

"Aye. I like your arse too much to let you damage it."

On shaky legs, she followed my lead, her body wobbling as I held her up.

"That's it. One foot in front of the other. I'll do the rest."

By the time we got out onto the ice, the public session had begun, and it went from calm to a wee bit frantic before she let me lead her out onto the ice. A small child zinged past us, skating backward with a huge grin on his face. He couldn't have been more than five.

Becca followed him with her gaze, which of course, took her away from mine. That was the moment I nearly lost her. Except the only sting she would feel on her pert arse would come from my palm. "Oh my God, it's so slippery." She wobbled, and I locked my stare on hers, keeping her upright.

"Yes, it *is* ice."

"How do you do this?"

"Well, the first thing you need to know is you have to practice. It's normal to fall. It's normal to lose your balance to end up arse over teakettle more than once."

"What if I don't want to fall?"

"You have me. That's what I'm here for." I spun and positioned myself in front of her, holding both her hands while I skated backward and pulled her along. She kept looking down and tilting forward, losing her balance.

"Don't look at your feet. Look at me. Look into my eyes."

She gave up her control, her balance righting itself.

"You want to stay centered on the blade. Too far forward and you'll tip too far to either side. Your feet will come out from under you. Glide."

She took a deep breath and gripped my hands tight. "Glide. Okay."

"I can guide you. You're doing really well."

"Am I?"

"Aye. You're doing better than I did my first time out."

"You were two."

"I was. Can you just take the compliment?"

"Sorry. Yes, thank you."

We skated together for an hour until she was doing it on her own. She only fell one time, but it was a doozy. She took me with her, legs sliding out underneath mine and collapsing. I used my body to break her fall. There was no way she'd get hurt on my watch. By the time we were unlacing our skates, she was grinning widely, her nose pink from the cold.

"That was really fun."

Fuck, I loved her smile. "Wanna grab some dinner?"

"Yeah. Yeah, that sounds really nice."

"Good. I wasn't ready to let go of you just yet."

"If I'd known you were this guy when we met on the ferry, I think I would have given you more of a chance."

"Why didn't you think I was this guy?"

"You laughed at me and told me I was Tinkerbell."

"I laughed with you because you were the cutest thing I'd ever seen. And you do remind me of her."

She scrunched up her nose in the most adorable fucking way. "I think you're . . . I don't know. I don't know what I think. You're—"

"Handsome. The word is handsome. It's okay. You can say it." I flashed her a wicked grin.

She laughed. "Yes, handsome. But also charming. Sexy. All of those things, but also, I think . . . cute. You're really cute."

"Cute? Cute is for pixies, not for pirates."

"You're not a pirate."

"Who says? You?"

"Yes."

"Maybe you didn't understand me the first time. I am Captain Hook, not Peter Pan."

"Well," she twirled a length of her hair between her fingers. "Maybe I'd like to spend a little time with the pirate."

"Oh, lass, that can be arranged."

"So is this really your usual date? Ice skating

and hand-holding don't really seem like your style,"

"Oh, lass. You wound me. I am as swoony as they come. It's just been a while since I had to . . ." I raked a hand through my hair.

"Work for it?"

"Aye."

She laughed and shook her head. "Athletes."

"What?"

"You're all so cocky, so confident. You think that just because you hit a little puck across some ice we're all going to roll over and spread our legs for you."

The thought of her doing just that sent a bolt of need straight to my cock. "No one asked you to do that. Unless I said it without thinking? Is there some kind of secret code I'm not aware of?"

"Nope. No secret code." She waved her fingers at my face. "It's all here."

"That's just my face. If you've got a problem with it, take it up with my mum. My dad's a real wanker, though, so I doubt he'd talk to you."

"Why? Am I not good enough?"

That cut me. "Why would you ever say that? He doesn't deserve to breathe the same air as you."

Her eyes widened. Fuck, I'd scared her.

"You . . . really don't like him, do you?"

I shrugged, my chest tightening at the thought of my family. I wasn't ready to talk about them with her. I never discussed Dad if I could help it. "So are you ready to crack on with this date, then?"

She linked our hands, smiling up at me with the sweetest bloody look on her face. "I thought maybe we were done. You've been with me for the better part of the day."

What was she on about? I wasn't nearly done with her. She captivated me. There was no denying it. "I don't think I'll ever be ready to let you go. You're far too sweet, and I've got a soft spot for sweets, lass." She tilted her head, grinning. Fuck, her lips looked like pink candy, like they'd taste like candy floss or bubble gum.

"What makes you think I'm sweet? Haven't I proven the opposite?"

I took a chance, sliding my hand around her nape and tugging her close. "Well, perhaps this is my chance to test my theory."

"Perhaps."

I dropped my head, bringing my lips close, just barely touching hers. Then I whispered, "Sweet. I can sense it."

Before I could well and truly kiss her, she tilted her chin up and did it for me. Her mouth was soft and plump, warm and yes . . . sweet. Her little moan went through me, collecting at the base of my spine and sending arousal through me. She tasted like . . . cardamom?

Oh, fuck.

"What kind of lipstick is that?"

I backed away, already feeling my lips tingle from contact with the one fucking thing I was allergic to. "Isn't it nice? It's a gloss my friend makes. She adds cardamom extract. It gives it such a unique flavor, but . . . Um, Taylor, you don't look so good."

"I need my knapsack."

"What?"

"Now."

Her eyes widened. "Are you allergic to cardamom?"

Intense itching spread across my face as my skin reacted. Bloody hell, I wasn't prepared for this. Who puts cardamom in their fucking lipstick?

"Oh my God, are you going to die? Your lips are all puffy. Your face is red and splotchy."

I shook my head. "Not if you get my EpiPen out of the back of the car." I fumbled in my pocket for my keys and tossed them at her. Trying to keep my cool as my throat began to itch.

Becca ran around the car and popped the boot open, each second that passed causing the building panic to heighten. But then she returned brandishing the lifesaving medicine. As though she'd done this before, she popped the cap and stabbed me hard in the thigh. Then she took my hand and dragged me to the passenger side of the car, opening the door and shoving me inside.

"What are you doing?"

"Taking you to the hospital. Maybe I should call an ambulance?"

I shook my head. I was already feeling better; I didn't need an ambulance, but the fear in her eyes was enough for me to agree as she slid into the driver's seat and started up the engine.

"Just take me home."

"Your lips are swelling. And your cheeks too. You look like a chipmunk."

Now that she mentioned it, I felt pretty rotten. My lungs hurt and my head was fuzzy.

"Okay. Yeah. Hospital. That's a good idea."

At least I could breathe. For now.

I closed my eyes, and before I knew it, she was unloading me into a wheelchair and rushing about, barking orders at a nurse as I watched on in amazement. Sure, I was moments from passing out, but bloody hell, she was a fierce beauty.

"You're all mine," I murmured as she stared down at me once I'd been doped up and was safely in a hospital bed.

"I think you might be more trouble than you're worth, Taylor Savage."

"Or maybe I'm just the right amount."

She chuckled and sat on the edge of my bed, holding my hand. "You might be right."

4

BECCA

Taylor's apartment was right in the city center. Not the top floor, but close, in a skyscraper I'd never even realized people lived in. When we got to the hallway, his eyes were drooping, fatigue clear on his face. He might not want to admit it, but whatever they'd given him at the hospital was doing a number on him now.

"Give me your key, Taylor," I murmured, putting his arm over my shoulders and wrapping mine around his waist.

"I'm fine, lass. I promise. You don't have to help me."

"I'm not helping you. I'm cold, and you're keeping me warm. There, does that make you feel better?"

A low rumbled laugh escaped him as he fished

in his pocket and finally produced the keys I had returned after parking his car.

"Which one is it?"

He gestured lazily to the door at the end of the hall.

"Of course it's all the way down the hall."

"Corner view. I can see the whole city. At least the parts I want to see."

"Athletes. All that money and you don't know what to do with it aside from showing off."

"I know exactly what to do with it. Don't judge me because I have a nice place to live."

Chastened, I ducked my head and muttered an apology. "You're right. I shouldn't begrudge you the finer things in life."

"No, you shouldn't, especially when I'm about to share them with you."

"Oh no. I'm not being reeled into your trap."

"What trap?"

"You're gonna lure me into your lair and then . . ."

"What?" He nuzzled my neck with a lazy chuckle, whispering over my skin. "Ravish you?"

"Exactly."

I knew, though, that nothing would happen tonight. Taylor Savage was going to pass out the moment his head hit the pillow. I told myself I would just get him inside and make sure he was okay. Ensure he had everything he needed since I was the one who tried to murder him. Then we could go our separate ways.

"Come on, Tink. Are you really so afraid of me?"

"I'm not afraid of you."

"That's a lie."

It might be, but I wasn't going to tell him that. The truth was, he gave me the flutters. No one had given me the flutters in a long time.

I finally got the door open, which wasn't as easy as it should have been because I had a big, bulky Scot draped over me who was getting heavier by the minute. Flipping the lights on when I went inside, I smiled at the simple, clean lines of the place. An open floor plan, wall-to-wall windows, and, as promised, a view of the best parts of the city.

"Aren't you afraid people are gonna look in your windows?"

He chuckled. "They cannae see in. Only I can see out."

"Are you sure about that?"

"Aye, lass, I'm sure. I paid extra."

"It's beautiful."

"I know."

"Where's your bedroom?

"Oh, she moves fast. Are you sure you don't want me to press you up against those windows and—"

"Stop right there. You're in no shape to do any

kind of ravishing. Against the windows. In your bed. On the kitchen counter."

"Kitchen counter. Now that's a good suggestion."

I rolled my eyes. "Taylor, come on."

I dropped the white pharmacy bag on the coffee table as we passed by. Then I followed his directions down the hall, past two other doors, until reaching his bedroom. I'd expected the same masculine, modern design, but instead I was greeted with a bed that looked soft as a cloud, a thick white rug at the foot, and photos hanging on the walls. A chair in the corner was covered in laundry—but it was folded.

"This is cozy."

I could hear the smirk. "Makes you want to stay, doesn't it?"

"No, Taylor, we are not sleeping together tonight."

"Yes, we are."

"No, we're not."

"Come on. I didn't say anything about fucking. I don't want to be alone. I have a headache. And . . . you did nearly kill me."

"You are the worst."

"You like it, though."

I laid him down on the bed. His eyes closed, lips already back to normal. He rested one palm on his stomach, and the other slid down my arm until he grasped my wrist, his thumb gently running across the underside.

"Just stay with me, lovely. For a while."

Why did that get me? What was it about his vulnerability? Inwardly I groaned. His gentleness hit me right in my weak spot. That was why. Give me a man who wasn't afraid to admit he needed something. A man who could be open with me. Who didn't feel like he was putting on a show most of the time we were together. That's who Taylor had been. Occasionally his facade of big bad cocky athlete slipped through, but for the most part, he'd been this version. The man I wanted.

A tendril of fear unfurled in my gut. But what if *that* had been the facade? What if he read me like a book and knew exactly how he needed to act to get me to want to be with him so he could get me in bed?

Stop it, Becca. You're self-sabotaging.

I was. I was very good at that. But my examples for most of my childhood of what made a healthy relationship were sorely lacking until my sister Clara met and married Maverick Wilde. I hadn't seen happiness, respect, or real love until them. Was it too much for me to hope I would find that? It seemed unlikely. A love like Maverick and Clara's only came around once in a lifetime.

"Lass?" Taylor murmured, fading fast. His

voice pulled me from my panic spiral. "Lie with me or leave me. Just don't keep me in suspense."

I should have left. I should have walked out the door and never looked back. Instead, I sighed and crawled onto the bed next to him. In one smooth move, he rolled over and spooned me. Holding me close, he inhaled deeply.

"You smell good. So fucking good."

He didn't try to feel me up or rock his hips into mine. He just laid there with his face buried in my hair and one arm around my waist as he drifted off to sleep. I stared at the room, listening to the sounds of his even breaths. Weirdest first date ever.

I woke with a heavy arm draped across my waist, the scent of Taylor Savage sending arousal through me. God, the man was sexy as fuck.

"Don't you move, lass. I'm comfortable. If you leave me, I'll be cold, and you'll have something else to feel guilty for."

I let out a soft giggle. "That line is getting old."

"You're right. It's outlived its usefulness."

"Ah, so you admit you were using it to your advantage. Milking it for all it was worth."

"It worked, didn't it?" He tightened his hold on me, tugging me into his body.

"Looks like it."

"Are you hungry?"

"Are you really offering to feed me breakfast?"

"Of course I am. Coffee too."

I snuggled into him, the deep groan that rumbled from his chest making me shiver with longing. "I'm a lover of coffee."

"Mmm. I'd rather you be a lover of me." And then there was the hard ridge of his erection pressed against my ass.

Wow. There was potential for significant damage to be done if he knew how to use that thing.

His lips trailed over my shoulder, the rough brush of his stubble scraping along my skin making me rock back into him.

"Careful, lass. You'll make me forget my manners."

I moaned, my breath catching as his palm drifted up between my breasts and his teeth grazed the tender skin of my neck. "What if I don't want you to have good manners? Aren't you the Scottish bad boy? Be bad with me for a minute."

He grunted and thrust his hard dick into me. "I'll need a lot longer than a minute to show you what I can do."

"I don't have anywhere to be."

"I thought you didn't want to sleep with me."

"We already broke that rule. I woke up in your

bed. Besides, I never said I didn't want to fuck you."

The rough groan he released as he cupped my breast and bit down on my earlobe had need shooting straight to my clit. "Fuck me, lass. You cannae say things like that to me and expect me to keep myself under control."

"Who says I want you to?"

"You're so soft and sweet."

That made heat creep across my skin. I was soft. Curvy. The opposite of the women most athletes dated. The mention of my curves had me tensing.

"What's this? What just happened?" he asked, continuing to kiss a line up my neck.

His palm left my breast and trailed down to my belly, a place I'd always been self-conscious of. Again, I flinched, grabbing his hand and trying to keep him from touching me there.

"Tink . . . are you trying to hide your gorgeous fucking curves from me?"

"They're not gorgeous."

He rolled me over so I was facing him. God, the man was so handsome I could barely breathe. He stared me down, eyes filled with intense hunger. "You are the most beautiful creature I've ever seen. All of you. Your curves, your smart mouth, the freckles across the bridge of your nose. All of you."

Fuck. Tears burned in my eyes. Was this cocky puck boy making me cry with his sweet words?

I sat up. "Stop it, Taylor."

He followed. "Stop what? Telling you the truth? If you can't see how stunning you are, you need someone to do it for you."

"I don't look like them."

His brows pulled together. "Them? Who is them?"

"The women you date."

Lips pressed into a tight line, he waited for me to elaborate.

"I looked you up. You date models and actresses. Not full-figured bakers."

"And I haven't spent more than a night with any of them, Becca. But you? There's something special about you." A spark of fear flickered in his gaze. "Fuck. There is. Nothing has ever felt as real as this."

I bit my lower lip. "Taylor."

"Don't tell me no, Becca. I can't take it if you do."

Whatever happened after this, I couldn't say no now. Not when I felt the same sense of rightness he did. It might've all been an act, but I didn't give a single fuck. Right now, Taylor and I were here, together, and I would be real for him. I'd give him everything until I woke up and the dream faded into reality.

"I'm not saying no."

"Thank fuck."

TAYLOR

God, but she was a beauty in every sense of the word. Everything about Becca Barnes, except for her choice of lip gloss, was beautiful. There was nothing more perfect in this world than waking up with her in my bed, except maybe being inside her. That might be the best thing I could think of.

"I'm not saying no." Her whisper made my cock jerk, a deep ache building in my balls.

"Thank fuck."

Leaning in, I stopped myself before I gave in and kissed her. She must've seen my hesitancy because she smiled.

"I washed it off my lips and tossed the deadly gloss in the garbage at the hospital."

I kissed her long and slow, savoring her, drinking in the soft little noises she made as my hips fit into the cradle of her thighs and I rocked against her.

"Why are we wearing so many clothes?" I groaned, my fingers trailing down her body until

I found the hem of her shirt. "I want to feel your skin. It's so soft. So silky."

She kissed the tender spot just under my ear. Her small hitched gasps in response to my touches had me rolling my hips, grinding against her.

"We'll only take this as far as you want, lass. You're in charge."

Wrapping her legs around my waist, she threaded her fingers in my hair and tugged as she bit down on my ear. I wanted her so fucking badly I was shaking from the effort not to tear off her clothes and sink into her all the way.

"Touch me, Taylor. Please. Make me feel good. It's been so long."

I couldn't keep from moving my hand down, under the waistband of her pants, to the already wet cleft between her thighs. Not when she asked so sweetly. I gave her exactly what she wanted.

"So you are desperate with wanting me, then? Because I am. I've been dying to feel you since I saw you on that blasted ferry."

"You're a talker. Why am I not surprised?"

She reached down and grabbed my length without warning. Fireworks. Fucking fireworks.

"So are you. Oh . . . God, keep doing that."

"You don't want me to talk?"

"No, I want you to cry out my name as you come all over my fingers so I can lick them clean."

She continued stroking me slow and steady,

her hum of pleasure urging me on as I toyed with her swollen clit.

"Does that feel good, lass? Tell me I'm giving you what you want."

"More. Inside me, please."

Her breathy plea had my own release on the edge of spilling over. I dipped my fingers inside her heat, the tight clench of her slick muscles around me as my thumb continued working her small button of pleasure.

"Fuck, you're drenched."

"Your cock is so thick."

"Sweet talker."

"It's never going to fit. I've never been with someone so big."

Jesus, I was going to come all over her hand before we could test that theory. "You've never been with someone like me." I stared into her eyes and watched as she came. She fell over the cliff and shuddered, eyes fluttering closed.

"God, Taylor."

"Fuck, if you don't stop . . ." My words cut off on a groan as I did exactly what I had been worried about. I rocked into her hand, chasing every wave of pleasure as I came.

"What was that?" The teasing tone made me even harder.

Pulling my fingers from her cunt, I brought them to my mouth and sucked her arousal off each digit. Her eyes were hooded and everything relaxed in her, a sexy smile playing on her lips.

"I knew you'd taste fucking good."

She let out the cutest giggle, then brought her palm to her lips, bringing my erection back in full force as she licked my cum off her skin.

"Same."

"Fuuuuck, lass. Are you trying to kill me?"

"I hope you're hydrated, Taylor."

I kissed her again before opening her jeans and pulling them down her hips. My cock throbbed again, reminding me he was ready to put my stamina to the test.

"Do you doubt me?"

"It's been a rough twenty-four hours. I wouldn't hold it against you if you had to tap out."

Letting out a low growl, I nipped her neck. "Is that a challenge?"

She gripped my shirt and tugged until I couldn't ignore her silent request. I helped her remove the fabric, baring my body to her and loving the way she took in my ink with awe on her face.

"You're beautiful."

The way she breathed the compliment, as though she hadn't expected it, made me proud. Hands that were hungry for my cock now explored the intricate designs covering my chest.

"How many do you have?"

Her fingers slid down my abs and over my hipbones, following the lines of black ink until she reached my waistband. I needed her to keep up her exploration, to build this connection that was weaving between us.

"They mostly all blend together now, part of a bigger design, but I'd say thirty, maybe forty at this point."

"That's a lot of pain."

"You don't have any?"

"No."

I smirked. "Do you want any?"

"Maybe. But right now, I just want you."

I sat up on my knees before shoving my joggers down, then I freed my length and gave myself a long stroke as she watched.

"Your turn to show me yours, hen."

She giggled. "Hen? Did you just call me a chicken?"

"Aye, I suppose I did. It's a term of endearment, trust me."

When she bit her lower lip and hooked her thumbs under her knickers, I had to hold my breath to keep from reaching for her and helping the process along.

Banging on the front door echoed through the flat, causing Becca's breath to catch in her throat and, more importantly, stopping the show she was putting on for me.

"Savage? You alive in there? Open up!"

"Who is that?" Becca hissed, rolling out from under me and grabbing her jeans.

"A dead man," I muttered.

But the banging started again, and I gritted my teeth against the frustration. I'd done it to myself.

"It's Trick. He's here for a workout. I'm sorry, hen. I forgot I had plans with him this morning."

I made quick work of changing out of my cum-stained joggers and into a pair of black athletic shorts.

Pinning Becca with a stare, I ordered, "Stay. Right. There. Don't move from this bed." I hoped she couldn't see the desperation in my eyes.

She nodded and stretched, arching her back and pressing her tits forward as she gave me a soft little moan.

"You're a fucking tease, that's what you are."

"Just doing my best to keep you coming back for more."

"Oh, aye, I'll come back. I'm already addicted."

As soon as I left the room, I missed her. God, the woman had me wrapped around her little finger already. That hadn't happened in . . . a long bloody time.

I was infatuated.

Trick hammered on the door again, and I yanked it open just in time for him to raise his fist again.

"Good God, man, haud yer wheesht! It's early

yet. I don't want my neighbors to hate me any more than they already do."

"You don't have neighbors. You made sure of that. Don't give me any of that Scottish bullshit your granny uses."

Trick was dressed for our run, with a gym bag slung over one shoulder, headphones around his neck.

"You're not ready. Fuck, man, did you forget?"

"Aye. I have a wee bit of a distraction in my bed at the moment."

He smirked. "A distraction? The hot kind?"

"The hottest."

"And I'm cockblocking."

"That's one way of putting it, aye."

"Then don't let me stop you. Looks like that dating app is working out great for you."

I wasn't sure what to tell him. I hadn't met her on the app. I hadn't even opened the fucking thing since I set up my account.

"Yeah. I've got them lined up round the block," I lied.

"Legend. Well, have fun getting your cardio in. Same time tomorrow? It's leg day."

I jerked my chin at him in agreement, then shut the door in his face. The last thing I wanted was to spend another minute away from the sweet pixie waiting in my bed. But she was dressed and standing in the doorway to my room when I turned around.

"Lined up round the block, huh?" Her eyes were narrowed, hands balled into tight fists.

"Don't be like that, hen. I was only having a laugh with him."

"At my expense?"

"Nae, that's not what this was."

She walked toward me, her syrupy sweet smile telling me I was in big trouble. "You know what? You're right. It's not what this was. You and I had a good time, and that's all. Thanks for the orgasm, Taylor. I'll see you around."

I reached for her, needing to pull her into my arms so I could kiss the sass right out of her, but she jerked away.

"No. I'm going home. Like I should have done last night."

"Come on, Becca. Give me a chance to prove it to you."

"The only thing you've proven was that you're the player I suspected you were from the start." Tugging open the door, she shook her head. "I'm not interested in that. I'm not someone you can toy with. Goodbye, Taylor."

She left me standing there, the echoes of her voice ringing in my mind, the sweetness of her perfume lingering in the air.

I pressed my palm to the doorframe and let her leave, determined to win her over and show her we'd be good together. One way or another.

"Fuck it," I muttered before running after her.

I caught the little blonde firecracker as she waited for the elevator. Her huff of annoyance would have made me laugh if I wasn't on the verge of losing any hope of something with her.

"Did you forget something?" She didn't even look at me.

"Aye, I did."

Twisting in my direction, she arched one brow. "What's that?"

"You."

"I already told you goodbye. You didn't forget anything."

"Becca, I'm sorry. I don't want this to be the end. You . . . you're not like other—"

"If you say I'm not like other girls, I'm going to kick you in the shin."

A bark of laughter escaped before I could stop it. "Do you have any idea how sexy you are?"

"I threaten to assault you, and you think that's sexy?"

"You challenge me."

"You deserve it."

God, this woman. I wanted to shake her and kiss her silly all at the same time.

"Aye, you're not wrong." The elevator arrived, announcing my time was up with a ding. The door slid open, and she walked into the car. Fuck. I couldn't let her go yet. I held the door in place, keeping it from closing. "Don't leave like this. Let me see you again. Let me show you I'm not a waste of your time."

I saw it the moment she let her guard down. She bit that sexy full bottom lip and took a slow breath.

"Maybe."

"Not good enough."

Her lips formed a little o of surprise. "Excuse me?"

"I want another go. I want a date."

"Nope. Not yet."

"You said yet. So you're saying there's a chance."

She grinned. "Maybe."

I hated that word.

"Fine. I'll take it."

The elevator tried to close on me again, but I held fast.

"Taylor, I need to go."

"I'm not giving up on you, Tink. That's a promise."

Pink bloomed on her cheeks. "We'll see."

Satisfied, I backed away and let her leave. But this time instead of a sinking feeling, I was filled with possibility and hope. I had a chance to make her mine. All I had to do was not fuck it up.

Easy.

5

BECCA

I spent the next three days reliving the morning with Taylor in my mind. Wondering what he was doing, if he'd fully recovered, if he was going to call. I hated it. I was not this person. This silly girl who waited on a man to make her feel important. And yet, here I was, checking my phone every few minutes. Desperate to hear from him.

Was it the toe curling orgasm? Probably. But also, I just wanted to hear his voice and let that deep rumbling laughter wash over me because I liked him a lot. I wasn't ashamed to admit it. I liked him more than I'd liked anyone, maybe ever.

"Becca, the timer has been going off! The cupcakes are probably dry and overbaked!"

Scarlett ran into the kitchen and pulled out the tray of cupcakes, which were, indeed, dry as a bone.

I sighed. "Sorry, I was distracted."

"I noticed. What's gotten into you?"

I wanted to say Taylor's tongue and fingers, but instead I shrugged and stood up straighter, brushing invisible crumbs off my apron. "I just didn't sleep well. A lot on my mind."

"Well, do you think you could put us making these cupcakes on your mind? We need thirty-five more monarch butterflies made out of gum paste, and unless you want to do that, I'm going to be busy."

I didn't want to do that. Sugar art was not my forte. Scarlett would hand-paint and mold the beautiful, delicate butterflies without any trouble. I, on the other hand, would have a terrible time of it. She handled the finer details. I handled the rest. It was a good partnership, and it worked. But only when I held up my end of the bargain.

"I got it. Don't worry."

She gave me a look I would have reserved for our older sister rather than her, the baby of the family, but Scarlett always took care of everyone. Me, Clara, our friends, she was the most together out of the two of us. And I thought part of that was due to necessity. Growing up as we had without parents for most of our lives, reliant on Clara to take care of us, we'd had to become self-sufficient.

My phone chirped from the counter, and I flinched as my heart took up a frantic pace.

"God, are you expecting a call or something? You just freaked the heck out."

"No."

"What is going on with you?" She narrowed her gaze. "Are you dating someone?"

"Maybe. Kind of. Not really. I don't know."

"Rebecca Anne, tell me."

I sighed heavily. "I went out with one of the guys on Clara's team?" I said it as a question, hoping that would soften the blow.

"Wait, a hockey player for the Cyclones?"

"Yeah. We met on the ferry a few weeks ago and kind of hit it off."

"Does he know?"

"What?"

"You know what. That your sister is the owner's wife."

"Yes, he knows. He doesn't care. And neither do I. I'm not affiliated with the team. I don't work for them. As far as we're concerned, we're just two strangers who met on the ferry. That's it."

She rolled her eyes. "Sure. That's what we're gonna call it. Strangers."

"There aren't any rules against it."

"No, there aren't. But it kind of muddies the waters, don't you think?"

Unease curled in my belly. She was right. It did. "Maybe."

"Did you... make love?"

"Scarlett!"

"It's an honest question."

"No, we didn't *make love*."

"Then why are your cheeks so red? And your ears? Your ears always go red when you lie."

"I'm not lying."

Her shrewd gaze raked over me. "Okay. Did he... did you show him... your treasure?"

"Oh my God, Scarlett. You are twenty-five years old. You really have to get over this aversion to body parts."

"I don't have an aversion. I just don't like to say crude words."

"This is what we get for putting you in the church daycare after school. Those nuns really did a number on you."

She shuddered. "They were scary. I still don't understand why I had to go to daycare and you didn't. You're not that much older than me."

"I was just old enough that I could participate in after-school activities. I didn't need extra supervision. But you, miss so shy she flinched away from a butterfly, couldn't handle anything. That's not my fault."

I sighed. My phone chirped again, and my

fingers itched with anticipation. I wanted to see who it was.

"Anyway, we're talking about your new life as a puck bunny. Tell me the rest."

I left the puck bunny comment alone and told her everything. "He took me home, and we did not make love. And yes, I let him see my treasure. Happy?"

She scoffed. "I can't believe you gave him your treasure."

"Scarlett, I did not give him my treasure. I just let him play with it."

"Oh my gosh, you're very naughty." She threw a small glob of white buttercream at me, hitting me on the arm.

So I did the same, hitting her in the shoulder. "And you are very nice. Now can I please check my phone to see if he wants to go treasure hunting again?"

Her cheeks turned a deep crimson, the color rushing up her face and into her hairline. "I'll just go make some butterflies."

"Yes, that sounds like a fantastic idea."

As she walked away, I grabbed my phone, flipped it over, and immediately deflated at the sight of my best friend Elles' name on the screen.

Elles: What are you doing tomorrow?
Me: Apparently I'm hanging out with you.
Elles: <smiley face>
Me: What's wrong?

Elles: I need a distraction.

Me: From?

Elles: Everything.

Me: Okay. I have to find a dress for this stupid charity function I'm going to. Do you want to go shopping with me? Do a preliminary run?

Elles: That sounds great.

Me: I'll meet you in the city tomorrow.

Elles: Great, I'll see you there.

The next day, after shopping with Elles and watching her flirt like crazy via DM with her mystery man on *Meet-Cupid,* she and I headed to the wine bar around the corner. I didn't get to see her enough, not with how busy we were at the shop.

"So what's going on with the bakery? When are you moving in?" Elles asked as she brought her wineglass to her lips.

"We're trying. The kitchen is a disaster."

"Really?"

I swirled my wine in the glass, the red liquid sloshing up the sides, then trailing down in slow legs. "Yeah. It was my fault. Scar signed the lease without me because I was late. She accepted it as-is."

"Didn't you know there were problems?"

"No. On the surface, it looked fine. Until we went in and took possession. Pretty much every single piece of equipment needs replacing."

"Fuck."

"Yeah."

"That sounds expensive."

"It is. We're working on it, but it'll be a few months before we can open."

"Can you keep it going? The rent and running the shop out of your garage?"

The question made my chest tight. "For now. I need to get things moved over sooner rather than later, though."

"You know I'll design it for you, right? No charge."

I smiled at her. "I know."

"You can pay me in cupcakes."

"Perfect."

TAYLOR

I scrolled through the Meet-Cupid app at Eva's request, familiarizing myself with everything I was supposed to be representing. Myself, Byrne, Trick, Petrov, and Reuben had all gotten roped into this. And today after practice, Eva strode into the locker room ready to all but hand us our arses. Determination burned in her eyes, and from the set of her jaw, I could hear her voice in my head like a fucking Banshee even before she opened her mouth.

"We won't keep our sponsorship if you don't use the app, and I will find myself another team to support. Don't test me, boys. This is my first big sponsorship opportunity for you guys. You're as good as brand new to the NHL."

None of us were fucking new. We'd all been on other teams. Hell, this team wasn't brand new. We just had a new owner. I almost piped up. Almost told her she needed to simmer down and let us do our thing. But that woman was scary.

As if she knew what was going on in my head, she lasered her gaze on me, and I all but withered. Byrne laughed under his breath.

"What's so funny, Ethan? You're just as bad. The only ones here who have even fully set up their profiles are Savage and Reuben. Although, Taylor, your bio is pathetic."

"What? I've just given the ladies what they want."

She pulled out her phone and began reading. "They don't call me number 10 for nothing. Taylor 10-inch Savage at your service, lassies."

Everyone in the locker room snickered. "See? It's good." I puffed out my chest in defense of my smart mouth.

"No. It's something a chauvinist pig would write. You're representing the Cyclones, especially since you're using your real name. Unlike others." She shot a pointed look at Ethan, who simply shrugged. "You're changing it once we go live. Once the promo is out."

He shrugged again.

"See, love? You have to like me better than that tosser."

"I like all of you the same, which is to say not at all. You're all like my children. Sticky, smelly, and annoying."

I leaned close to Petrov, whispering, "She has children?"

The big Russian shook his head in warning.

"I have to get reports to *Meet-Cupid* by this Friday. That means you only need to be using the app. They're tracking how much you interact. They're watching to see if this is working. Don't fuck this up."

"Miss Eva, ma'am." Trick raised his hand like we were in grammar school. I let out a disgusted laugh. What a wanker.

"Patrick, yes?"

"I just, um, are we supposed to have sex with these women?"

Her eyes went wide, and she choked on her own spit for just a moment but recovered. "Patrick, I don't care what you do with your dick. If you like the girl and want to sleep with her, great, but you don't have to. You're not being paid to sleep with them. That's illegal."

"Right?" He asked it like a question rather than a statement.

"Okay, good."

"Great."

I stared at the man, my brow furrowing. Was our little Trick a virgin? No . . . Maybe . . . Interesting. I filed that little nugget of information away for future use. A virgin. Huh. Who would have thought? He was handsome. Not as handsome as me, but who was? He had a certain all-American charm. Kind of like if Captain America was a hockey player from the Midwest.

"Don't worry, Trick. No one's gonna tell your mommy."

Petrov nudged me and grunted.

"Oh, come on. It was too good to resist."

The soft tap tap tap of Eva's stiletto on the tile floor echoed in the room. "Are you finished?"

"Aye, I am."

"Good. Get on the app. Go on some dates. Post on social media. Get us paid."

I offered her a mock salute, then stood. "If that's all, I suppose I have a date waiting to be found."

She smirked. "That's a good boy."

Eva left, and the rest of the team began packing up, ready to leave for the day. I didn't want to be on the app. I wanted to be on my little Tink. I couldn't get the taste of her out of my mind. I swear the smell of her was still all over my sheets, even though that was impossible.

I pulled my phone from my pocket. The app was still open, and I rolled my eyes as I deleted my bio and updated it.

Bad boy looking for his good girl. Are you the pixie that's going to straighten out this pirate?

Then I opened my text messages and called up her name. She hadn't let me take a picture of her yet, so I'd used a screenshot of Tinkerbell, which made me grin like an idiot.

Me: What are you doing right now?

Tink: Having a drink.

Me: Where?

Tink: At a bar in the city.

She was here? Possibly close by.

Me: Which one?

Tink: Wouldn't you like to know?

Me: Aye, lass, I would. That's why I'm asking.

Tink: I'm with my friend.

Me: Is this a friend of the male persuasion?

Tink: Why? Are you jealous?

Me: Yes.

Tink: Oh . . .

Me: You want me to be jealous?

Tink: No.

Me: Does he know?

Tink: Does he know what?

Me: What your little cunt tastes like?

Tink: No.

Me: Then I'm not jealous. Where are you? I need to see you.

She sent me the address, a place not too far from the stadium. I breathed a sigh of relief. She hadn't shut me down.

Me: I'll be there in fifteen minutes.

Tink: I'll see if I can stick around.

Me: You fucking better.

Tink: Bring me the British one or no dice.

Me: What?

Tink: The Brit. Then I'll stay.

I bristled. Why did she want Ethan? But there was no way in hell I'd let that keep me from having time with her.

But then another text came through, and I relaxed.

Tink: I'm with my sister. Not some guy. If I'm going to be on a date, I want you to bring one for her so she's not the third wheel.

I glanced around and saw Byrne staring down at his phone, a fucking ridiculously dopey smile on his face. "Oh, shit, it's Big Deck Energy. He's in love, lads." I tossed a towel at his head. "Look at him, grinning like a wee little child looking at something he shouldn't."

"Give it a rest, Savage." He threw the same towel back at me, hitting me in the face.

"Come on, then. Give us a little bit. You refused to go out with us, won't let me set you up with my girl's friends. That must mean you found yourself a bonnie wee lass."

"You don't say bonnie wee lass. You haven't even been home to Edinburgh in fifteen years. You only put on the accent that thick when you want something. Spoiler alert, it doesn't work on me. I don't have a thing for drunk Scots."

"Maybe you're right, but I do have a thing for making my girl happy. And she wants a double date tonight."

"No, thanks. I'm not keen on being a third."

I laughed and clapped him on the shoulder. "Come on. I told her I'd set up her sister, and she said, and I quote, 'bring me the British one or no dice.'"

"Well, I guess it's no dice. Cheers, mate."

Byrne stood and stripped down before walking to the showers. He'd come around. He owed me. So I got cleaned up and waited, snagging his phone while I was at it. It seemed our resident Sassenach had a real thing for red lipstick.

"What?" he asked when he emerged.

"Oh, nothing, but . . . you really shouldn't leave your phone lying around. And on *Meet-Cupid* no less. Who is Elles?"

"I'm going to kill you."

I smirked as I recalled the updated profile bio I'd given him while he was showering.

Professional knobhead, has a shamefully small

willie but is surprisingly good with his tongue. Come on, lassies, have pity on this poor sod.

"Are you fucking kidding me?" My smile only grew as he tapped the screen and his brows drew together. "Savage, you fucking changed my password? How did you know what it was in the first place?"

"You are nothing if not predictable. Now if you want to know how to change it back..."

Ethan sighed. "Fine. I'll go with you. But one Harry Potter reference, and I'm out of there."

"I just need you for five minutes."

"Five?"

"Five. Just enough time to prove to her I'm good on my word, and then you can go."

Fifteen minutes later, Byrne walked through the pub door and joined the girls and me.

"There he is! Byrne, get over here, you sad excuse for a center." I held out a pint for him, hoping he realized how important this was to me.

"All right, all right, I'm here. You don't have to announce it to the world, mate."

"This is Scarlett. My Becca's little sister."

"By one year. I'm not that much older than her,"

"And just to be clear, that age is over twenty-one since you're here in a pub, yeah?" Byrne grumbled the question like the old codger he was.

"Oh, come on, old man."

"I'm twenty-six, Scar's twenty-five,"

"Do you need to see my ID?" Scarlett asked, a teasing note in her voice.

"Nah, I'm good. Just making sure. You never know these days."

"So you're a center?" Scarlett's question was sweet and innocent, but Byrne couldn't have been less interested.

"Yeah."

"Cool. I don't know a lot about hockey. Just enough to get by when Clara invites us to games."

"Clara?"

"Our older sister," Becca supplied.

"As in Clara Wilde? The owner's wife?" He cut me a glance, and guilt hit me hard.

"Yeah. She invites us to their box all the time. Becca never goes, but I saw you play last week. You were so good out there. Really . . . fast." Scarlett smiled at him.

Byrne's glare could have melted me on the spot. "Can I speak to you for a moment?"

"I'm all ears."

"Outside."

"Fine, *Dad*. I'll be back, lass. Don't go anywhere."

Byrne turned on me the instant we were outside. "What the bloody hell do you think you're doing? The owner's *sisters-in-law*? Do you know how against the rules that is?"

"Technically it's not against any rule. They

don't work for the team. They're just . . . team adjacent."

"They're Clara's *sisters*."

"And they're fucking fit. Come on. You can't honestly say you wouldn't want to spend a day in bed with either of them."

"Yeah, I can."

"Your loss."

"I'm gonna head back. I've had quite enough of this blind date."

I shrugged. "Just as well. I got what I wanted. Becca will be pleased as punch I kept my promise, and that's all that matters. Maybe now she'll finally let me . . ."

"Wait, you two haven't?"

Fuck. How did I tell him she tried to send me into anaphylactic shock on our first date and Trick cockblocked me the next morning? "Nae, she's not like the rest. This one is a handful."

He smirked. "Sounds like exactly what you need. Someone to hand you your arse."

My stomach twisted at the thought. "You might be right."

"Just don't cock it all up, and you'll be fine."

"Easier said than done, mate. But I'll do my best."

By the time I got back into the pub, Becca and Scarlett were both standing with their purses over their shoulders.

"Whoa, where's the fire, ladies?"

Becca's steely glare sent ice through my veins. "I don't understand you, Taylor. Sometimes you're this sweet guy who's honest and open, and then other times you're... this. I like you, but I'm not interested in someone who can't figure out who he is. Call me when you've got your shit together."

Before I could stop her, she left me standing there with nothing to show for the night than a bar tab and three pints at an empty table.

6

TAYLOR

I swiped through profile after profile on the *Meet-Cupid* app. None of the women I'd matched with were appealing. But that wasn't their fault. It was because there was only one girl who had caught my eye. Becca. It probably didn't help that the Taylor Savage on the app wasn't even remotely who I really was. This persona I'd adopted long ago had never fully taken hold. And Becca only added to my certainty that I was done playing the part of the bad boy of hockey.

The team was on our way to Montana for a game against the Wildfire, then a team party at Wilde Horse Ranch hosted by Maverick. Trick was so excited to get a chance to ride a real horse, he was practically buzzing with anticipation. The guy was like a little kid. I'd never let him live it down.

Me? I was excited about one thing. Getting a chance to talk to Becca. To show her I was still in this.

I opened my text messages and stared at the two unanswered ones I'd sent her.

Me: This is me. Not giving up.

Me: Still here. Still thinking of you.

Honestly, I wasn't bothered. She would come around sooner or later. There was no denying our connection, the wild need, the pull we both felt toward each other. She liked me too much not to reply eventually. Jesus, I wasn't even thinking about her naked, and my dick stirred to life. The woman had no clue how much she owned me. Or did she?

Me: Okay, now you've got me begging. Please, sweetheart? Give me some shred of hope?

Three little dots appeared on the screen. God, I was pathetic. My stupid heart flipped. She was writing back. Finally.

Tink: What are you doing?

Me: Showing you I'm a man of my word.

Tink: You are persistent.

Me: When I want something, I go after it. All the way.

Tink: I'm not sure I should let you in.

Me: Why not?

Tink: You're too charming. You scare me.

I scared her? That was news to me. She bloody well terrified me. The way I wanted her—needed her—sent me off the edge every time I thought about what that meant.

Me: Someone told me if it doesn't scare you at least a little, it's not worth doing.

Tink: Friends.

Me: What?

Tink: We can be friends. That's what we should be before we are anything else.

She wanted to be my fucking friend?

Me: So you regularly let your friends make you come?

She didn't respond. So . . . I kept going, persistent arse that I was.

Me: Do you fantasize about taking your friend's clothes off with your teeth? Or laying them out across your dining room table and making a feast of them?

Tink: Taylor . . .

Me: Call me, lass. I need to hear you say you don't want this.

Tink: I can't.

Me: Why not?

Say it. Tell me it's because you do *want this.*

Tink: My sister is next to me.

Me: I'm on a bus full of hockey players. I don't care if they know I've got a hard-on as big as the fucking Space Needle.

My phone rang and I answered immediately.

"Took you long enough, hen."

"Friends don't dirty talk each other, Taylor."

"I'm not your friend."

"I need you to be."

I sighed. "Why are you so afraid to give me a chance?"

"Because I can see it from a mile away. You'll break me."

"No, I won't."

"That's what they always say."

God, I wished I could see her face. Touch her. Show her how much I wanted her.

"When I get back from this away game, let me take you out. We can be more than friends if you just let me show you that I'm a good man, regardless of what the tabloids say."

She let out a heavy breath, then hummed softly. "Come over for dinner. You, me, and Scarlett. I need a Savage buffer. You turn me into a hormonally charged teenager when we're alone."

I loved knowing she couldn't trust herself around me.

"Fine. I'll be there. Just tell me when."

"Friday evening? I have a client I need to make a delivery for in the late afternoon, then I'm all yours."

"Done. I'll see you then, lass."

"Taylor?"

Fuck, I loved the way she said my name.

"Aye?"

"Don't prove me right about you."

"I won't. I promise."

"Y'ALL LOOKED REAL GOOD OUT THERE," MAVERICK said as the team gathered on the wide cement patio that served as the Wilde's entertainment area. Apparently the main house at Wild Horse Ranch wasn't used anymore now that their dad had died. The Wildes rented the space for events and weddings instead. They'd chosen to keep their ranch going but lived out of their father's shadow. That was something I could respect.

"Aye, it was a good game." I tipped my whiskey to my lips, enjoying the flavor. It might not be true Scotch, but the Langston distillery knew what they were doing.

"How's the knee? You get it checked out?"

As if reawakened when he mentioned it, my knee gave a throb. "It's fine."

"That hit was pretty hard."

"I'm fine." I stood and walked to the bar, forcing myself not to limp or grimace. Then I filled my glass and returned. "See? No issue. Sometimes those hits look worse than they are."

He shrugged. "I guess you'd know better than me."

"Thanks for your concern, Mr. Wilde."

"Mav. Just Mav."

Mav's brothers and their wives were seated around the fire pit with the rest of the team, everyone chatting, laughing, and drinking. When Clara joined her husband, settling herself in Mav's lap, a pang went through me. She and Becca looked a lot alike. Down to their pretty smiles.

Fuck, I wanted Becca here with me. I wanted her in my arms, staring at me with that same kind of adoration. I wanted to make her smile like Mav did her sister.

"Is she finally asleep, baby?" he asked, placing a palm on Clara's denim-clad knee.

"Yeah. It was a fight, but she gave in eventually."

"Stubborn like her mama."

"I think it's her daddy who's the stubborn one."

He grinned up at her. "Maybe."

I chuckled, thinking of my first time minding my twin nephews as toddlers.

Mav cocked a brow. "That was the sound of someone with experience. You don't have kids do you?"

I shook my head. "No. I have nephews. Twin terrors. They might've been the reason that saying 'sleep is for the weak' was coined."

"I bet they have secret meetings and plot against us."

"Perhaps. They're cute little buggers, though."

"Is that something you want in the future? To settle down and have a family?"

Her question was gentle and honest, but my stomach churned. I hadn't thought too hard about it. "I don't really know."

The smirk on Mav's lips made Clara giggle. "Well, I can tell you from experience, it don't matter if you plan on it or not. When you meet the right one, you'll know. The only thing you'll want from then on is to be hers."

"Sometimes you're a real swoony bastard, you know that?"

Pride washed over him. "Isn't it why you fell for me in the first place?"

"Yeah. You're right."

"I just wish I hadn't wasted so much time not letting myself have you."

She kissed him softly. "We're making up for it now."

Settling back in my chair, I watched the stars twinkle across the vast expanse of the Montana sky and wondered if he was right. Had the right one come along already? Was I wasting time without her? But she wanted to go slow, be friends, take our time. That meant I had to play it cool and just be there until she realized we were more than that. She needed to know I was the right one for her. And I just had to prove it.

BECCA

"What do you mean Taylor Savage is coming over for dinner? I thought you weren't interested in him," Scarlett asked as she stared me down from across the prep table.

The two of us were working together, creating tiny fondant decorations for wedding cupcakes. We were working on handmade sugar flowers, then it would be time to decorate. This was one of the biggest events of our year, and the photographs would be shared on social media and in bridal magazines because this client was so high profile.

"I mean Taylor Savage is coming over for dinner."

"As in the hockey player? The same one we had drinks with?"

"Yeah."

"But he's a *hockey* player." My sister stared at me like I had lobsters crawling out of my ears.

"I don't see why that's a problem."

"You swore off athletes."

My chest tightened. Yes, my last serious boyfriend in college had hurt me. He'd been determined to go pro. Got drafted by the NFL. And then left me. But this was different. Taylor was already established in his career. He wasn't at the stage where he'd drop everything to get what he wanted.

"Yeah, I know that. I know. I just have to see this through. I can't explain it. There's just something really charming about him."

"Okay. If you like him, I'm sure I'll like him too. I just wish you'd told me you two started something."

"This is the first chance we've had to talk. We've been so busy."

I sighed. "We have. It's ridiculous. We live together. We should be able to talk whenever we want."

I agreed. She and I were like ships in the night because of how busy the bakery was. We needed to hire more staff. Hell, we needed a lot more than that.

"So what are we cooking him? We could make something fancy."

"I've got it covered." I grinned, finally letting myself feel that build of excitement at getting a chance to see him again.

A few hours later, Scarlett and I had put the finishing touches on the cupcakes, and I was buying fresh herbs for tonight's dinner. We only had a short stretch of time before delivery and set up for this wedding, and I had to make sure everything else was ready before Taylor came over. I had butterflies in my belly at the prospect of seeing him after our last text exchange.

My phone chirped from my back as I headed to my car with my bags in hand. Pulling out the device, I grinned when I saw he'd sent me a message.

Taylor: I'm sorry, lass. I can't make it tonight. Something came up. Forgive me?

Disappointment turned to a cold pit in my stomach. He wasn't coming? I had just spent an hour painstakingly choosing the ingredients for dinner. Made my famous apricot tart. And he wasn't coming?

Me: Oh, that's a bummer. Rain check?

The dots on the screen bounced up and down as he began typing a message.

Taylor: Really sorry. It couldn't be helped.

Me: I understand.

Taylor: I really want to get out of it.

Me: It's fine. Don't worry about it. You've got other things to do. I get it. I guess I'll just have to enjoy this delicious tart all by myself.

Taylor: Kicking a man when he's already down. That's harsh.

Me: If you really wanted it, I guess you'd be able to change your plans.

Taylor: Don't be like that. I really want to try your tart and see if it's as sweet as I think.

I rolled my eyes and sent him an emoji that did the same thing.

Taylor: Can you forgive me, lass?

Me: Fine. But you'll have to make it up to me. I was giving you a chance like you asked.

Taylor: I give you my word. I will make it up to you in a big way.

As I headed out to my waiting car, bag of groceries in hand, I let my frustration settle inside me. He said it couldn't be helped. That he couldn't get out of whatever obligation he'd been roped into. I couldn't build any kind of relationship with him if we didn't give each other the benefit of the doubt.

An hour later, Scarlett and I pulled up outside the wedding venue, a beautiful lodge nestled in the woods nearby. As soon as we arrived, the buzz in the air set my nerves on edge. Something was wrong. God, I hoped the wedding was still on.

"Oh, I'm so thankful you and your sister are here," Nora Winters said, rushing over to us. Her long beaded necklaces rattled like the chains of a ghost straight out of a Dickens novel.

"Hi, Ms. Winters. Where do you want the cupcake bar? The wedding cake is still in the truck."

Her usually breezy demeanor had vanished without a trace, replaced by an uptight stressed disaster. "Half the catering staff didn't show up. Apparently they got stuck in rush hour traffic. All lanes of I-5 are shut down due to an accident."

"Oh, that's terrible," Scarlett said.

"I don't know what to do. We have five hundred people showing up here in two hours. My daughter is getting her makeup done as we speak, and then they'll all be here for photos before the ceremony."

"We can help. If you want." Scarlett elbowed me in the side as I offered our services. "My plans for the night were canceled."

My sister frowned before throwing me a questioning gaze.

"Would you help? Oh, you two are just darlings. I promise I'll put you and the bakery in every single book I write from now on."

Honestly, we owed a lot to Nora. She'd been instrumental in helping us get our start. When she'd come to Bainbridge to spend six months writing her latest book, she happened upon our little bakery truck, and the rest, as they say, is history. She fell in love with the area, and it became an inspiration for her new series.

Scarlett and I finished setting up as the guests began to arrive, the caterers scrambling in the back but thankful we had dessert service covered.

"I need you to explain to me why we're here working when you were supposed to have a dinner date?" Scarlett asked as she placed a few plates on the table.

I shrugged, not wanting to admit I was disappointed. "He had to cancel. Something came up."

"Sure."

As the doors opened and the crowd filtered in, I took that opportunity to tear my attention from her and focus on the flowers adorning the table. They needed to be perfect. That was something I could control.

"Are you freaking kidding?" Scarlett muttered.

"What?"

"Something came up, I see." I followed her gaze to the table at the edge of the dance floor. The one with a tall, tattooed Scot seated next to a pretty little slip of a woman.

"Someone."

I dropped the cake knife with a loud clang, the sound drawing Taylor's attention. All the color drained from his face.

"Can we go?" I murmured as he stood and began striding toward me.

"Uh...No? We are sort of working here."

Taylor approached, his brows furrowed. "Hen, I know what this looks like—"

"You mean you choosing some supermodel at a high-profile wedding over me? Yeah. That's exactly what this looks like."

"It couldn't be helped."

I scoffed. "Oh yeah, I'm sure a hot date with her is such a hardship."

"Give me a chance to explain."

"You've had so many chances. This just isn't going to work."

He took my hand and pulled me around the table, then tugged me out of the room until we were in the quiet hall, away from the noise of the crowd and the music playing.

"Taylor, what are you doing?"

"I'm just talking to you, hen. I need you to understand what this is."

"I know. It's you on a date with another woman. Easy to parse out when it's staring me right in the face."

He shook his head. "No. That's not what this is. I'm doing my mate a favor."

This was such bullshit. "That's what we're calling it now? Taking a gorgeous woman on a date is a favor?"

"Hen—"

"Don't call me that."

"Becca. I don't even know her."

"That's just great." I ran my palms over my black apron.

"Reuben."

"I'm going to need you to give me more than that."

"My teammate? Tommy Reuben. He matched with Charlotte on the app and was supposed to come on this date with her. A big publicity thing for *Meet-Cupid*. But he had a full-on panic attack and called me. So I agreed to take his place. For the team."

My anger flickered out. "I . . ."

"Becca, I swear, I wanted to be with you. I'll come home with you right now if you want."

The way his jaw flexed had my heart hoping I could believe him, but I really didn't know. "No. You have obligations to uphold. You chose to take one for the team, so that's what you should do." I turned away from him, but he snagged me by the elbow. "Taylor..."

"This isn't over, hen."

"It never had a chance to start."

7

PRESENT DAY

BECCA

Taylor Savage was standing outside my house, shifting from foot to foot, holding a manila envelope. Why the hell was he here? I hadn't been in contact with him for months. This didn't make sense. He looked good enough to eat, though.

No. Stop it. He's not good for you.

I watched him from the path that led up to our front porch as he rang the doorbell and waited, his big body shivering.

Jogging back to the kitchen, I grabbed a few handfuls of sugar cookie dough and ran back to where I'd been standing.

"Bloody fucking hell," he muttered as he adjusted his cap and zipped his jacket.

When no one answered because I was right there, he shouted, "Becca, let me in, lass. I'm freezing my bollocks off out here."

I tossed the first glob of dough at him, hitting him in the back of the head. He turned, shock evident on his handsome face.

"Did you just assault me with . . . cookie dough, lass?"

"Yeah, I did. What are you going to do about it, Taylor?"

"That's a real waste. I thought you were meant to be a baker. Bakers . . . bake, don't they?"

Oh, that cocky smirk was going to be the death of me.

"Normally, yes, we do. This morning is an exception. What are you doing here?"

"I needed to see you."

"Why? We've said everything we need to say."

"No, we haven't."

"You could have texted me."

"Aye, but then you'd have been able to ignore me."

I assessed him, my eyes trailing his form until I stopped on the envelope in his hands. No, I could not deal with legal issues right now. Panic clawed at me. "Oh God. Are you suing me for some bullshit reason? Taylor, I can't afford to be sued. I'm barely keeping things going as it is."

"No, I'm not suing you. Why would I be suing you?"

Thank God. My relief was so palpable that I nearly wept. "Then why are you here?"

"Can we go inside? I'm fucking frozen."

"You're a hockey player. It's thirty-five degrees out here. Don't you have, like, superhuman powers of cold deflection?"

His chest got all puffed up as my comment landed. "While I love that you think I'm a superhero—"

"Villain."

"I'm not dressed like a hockey player. I still get cold. Besides, if memory serves, you like a bad boy."

He was so hard to resist. That was why not seeing him anymore had been my choice. I'd make stupid decisions if I spent time with Taylor.

"Let me in, lass. I need to ask you something."

"Fine. I was about to take a coffee break anyway. Follow me."

Taking him around the house, we walked past the former garage turned bakery, and he inhaled deep.

"How do you stand it?"

"Stand what?"

"Working in these conditions? I'd eat it all and never sell a single thing."

I shrugged. "I like money."

"Fair."

Scarlett was hard at work decorating a cake, unaware of the two of us as we walked by.

"This is where you bake everything? And you sell out of that little truck?"

"For now, yeah. We're leasing a space downtown, but our entire kitchen needs to be gutted and redone."

"Sounds expensive."

God, he didn't know the half of it. "It is." I leaned in through the doorway and called, "Scar! I'm taking a coffee break."

Scarlett gave me a curious glance before offering a thumbs up.

"Come on. Coffee's in the house."

As soon as we were in the kitchen, he heaved a sigh. "Thank fuck. Heat."

"You're a wuss."

"You're clearly a yeti. You're not even wearing a coat."

Grabbing two mugs, I decided to let the yeti comment go. "Cream? Sugar?"

"Just a bit of cream."

I motioned to the kitchen table, taking a seat as he followed suit across from me.

"So what in the world brings the bad boy of Seattle hockey to my doorstep at seven in the morning?"

Then he dropped a bomb on me. "I need you to marry me."

"I'm sorry, say that again?"

"You heard me. I need you to marry me. Today."

"Why would I do that? I don't even like you." I narrowed my gaze.

"Oh, come on, lass. You like me at least a little. You've let me put my tongue—"

As if in remembrance of his touch, my lady parts quivered. They *quivered*. "Stop right there. That was a mistake I made. I might like your tongue, but the man attached to it leaves a lot to be desired."

"What if I offered to pay for your new kitchen in exchange for your hand in marriage?"

"What is this, the Middle Ages? No."

"Just in name. We don't have to . . . you know."

"No, Taylor, I don't know. What in God's name could be so bad that you'd need a wife to get out of it?"

"Look, this app thing is getting out of control. They want me to be on some reality show next and to sign a five-year endorsement deal."

"Isn't that just money in your pocket?"

"No. I mean . . . it is, but it's also me being forced to use this bonkers app, date women I don't really like, then post about it, and, you know, sell my soul for profit."

I had no sympathy for the man's plight. "Aw, you poor baby. You're famous and being used by the big bad corporations for their financial gain. Must be hard."

"I'm serious, Becca. I'll pay for a state-of-the-art kitchen. I'll take care of you."

The absolute audacity of this man to come in here thinking I needed him to *take care of me*. So I told him exactly that. "I don't need you to take care of me."

"I know that. I just . . . I need help, and this is the only way I can get out of this bloody contract."

"How long?"

"What?"

"How long do we have to be married?"

"A year, just to be safe."

He had to be kidding. "An entire year? Are you crazy?"

"And we have to live together."

"What? You said in name only. I can't move off the island. I need to be close to the bakery. To Scarlett."

"I'll buy a house nearby. We can live there."

"Why do we have to live together?" I couldn't live with him. I'd fall for him if I had to see him every day, despite my better judgment.

"The contract with *Meet-Cupid* stipulates the agreement is void if I'm married and in a committed, co-habitant relationship."

Biting my lower lip, I let his offer sink in. Really sink in. I needed something to save us from this stupid decision we'd made, and I refused to ask my sister for her husband's money.

Would being Taylor Savage's wife really be the worst thing in the world? I'd get to look at him every day, smell that delicious cologne he wore, hear that Scottish brogue. And this would be good for the bakery. It would offer us financial security during our brick-and-mortar start-up years.

"You'll redo the kitchen exactly how we want it? No questions asked?"

"Aye."

"I get my own room?"

"Aye."

"One year living with you. Do I have to pretend to love you?"

"Only when we attend public functions. And we'll need to post on social media every now and then."

"But other than that, I can go about my life?"

"With the exception of dating. I can't have my wife dating other men."

"And you won't see other women." Well, at least we were on the same page there. I wasn't a sharer. Even if we weren't sleeping together.

"Aye, you'll be my moon and stars, lass."

"I don't see how we're going to do this today. We need a license, an officiant."

He placed the envelope on the table. "Taken care of."

Again, I say, audacity. He'd already had everything drawn up. "Are you serious? You knew I'd say yes?"

"I hoped so. You're a smart woman, business-minded, and even though you say you hate me, you don't really."

"I do."

"Look, you already know your lines."

I rolled my eyes. "Not helping your case, Taylor."

"Fine, hate me. But I need you to marry me tonight before the auction, love me or hate me."

"I suppose you've already booked an appointment at city hall too?"

He smirked, and I wasn't sure if I wanted to kiss him or slap him. "Aye. And I've got a suit in my car."

Taking a deep breath, I stared hard at the man I was about to marry. "What time is the appointment?"

TAYLOR

"Do you, Taylor Franklin Savage, take this woman to be your lawfully wedded wife . . ." The vows were a blur beyond these few sentences.

But it wasn't because I was scared. I was so stunned it actually worked. Becca Barnes had said yes. She'd agreed to marry me and live with me for the next year. Bloody hell, what had I gotten into?

"You are now husband and wife. You may kiss your bride," The Justice of the Peace grinned at me expectantly as I stared at Becca. Her cheeks were a faint pink, as though she'd never kissed me before.

She had. More than once. I'd left her breathless a time or two, in fact.

"What do you say, lass? Do you have a kiss for your husband?"

She bit her lower lip, then rose up on her tiptoes and pressed her mouth to mine. An instant rush of arousal hit me. She smelled like cookies, and it was one of the things I loved best about being near her. Becca was sugar sweet with a sharp bite to her if you weren't careful.

I backed away, grinning down at her. God, she was fucking adorable with her big blue eyes and the light spray of freckles across her nose she tried to hide with makeup.

"Are you sure you want to do this?"

She let out a sharp bark of laughter. "It's a little late now."

The Justice of the Peace snorted. "She's right."

That was it, the moment time stopped for

both of us. I saw it in her eyes. She felt it, the same as me. We'd done something we couldn't take back. Annulment, divorce, none of those things would change what we'd experienced here and now.

"Come on, lass. We have a marriage to celebrate."

I offered her my arm, and she frowned at me, giving me a long look before sighing and placing her palm on the crook of my elbow.

"Oh, what the hell. Take me home, husband."

I walked her out of the courthouse and back to my car, my nerves finally settling as she slid into the passenger seat and I rounded the arse end of the classic Corvette. Once I was seated, I took a deep breath and exhaled. "That was easier than I thought," I admitted.

"Did you think marrying me was going to be a chore?"

I laughed. "No. But I expected you to give me more trouble about it before agreeing."

She smirked. "Oh, don't worry. I'm sure I'll be more trouble than I'm worth before this year is up."

Starting up the engine, I smiled as my beautiful baby began to purr. "That's my girl."

"You have a weird attachment to this car."

"And you have a weird attachment to food."

She shrugged. "Fair."

I drove her home, my whole body feeling the weight of what I'd just done. I was fucking married. Sure, she'd already dumped me once, but that was fine. She didn't have to love me. She just had to tolerate me and be on my arm for every game, function, and public appearance for the next twelve months. There were worse things I'd dealt with than Becca Barnes. In fact, she was much more of a delight than she wanted me to believe.

"Are we debuting our newly minted status tonight at the auction?" she asked as I pulled into her driveway.

"Aye, lass. That's the whole reason for the rush."

"Then I guess I'd better cancel my *Meet-Cupid* date tonight."

I glared at her. "You'd better cancel any and all dates for the next three-hundred-and-sixty-five days, Mrs. Savage. You're mine."

"In name."

"In every way that counts. No one gets to touch what's mine. Not my skates, my stick, not my wife. Do you understand?"

She sighed and got out of the car. "Well, it's a good thing I have a great vibrator, then. It's gonna be a long year."

The mention of her playing with toys brought to mind all sorts of things I shouldn't be thinking. Me helping her with those toys. Her showing me how they worked. Us playing together.

Fucking hell, I had a cockstand the size of the Eiffel Tower, and if she looked my way before I could adjust myself, she'd know exactly what kind of lecherous prick I was.

"What are you doing?" she asked as I followed her to her door.

"I'm walking you home, then I'm gonna pop to the loo. And grab a bite before I head home."

"You don't have to walk me home."

"Aye, lass. I do. You're my wife now. That means I take care of you."

Her gaze shifted to me as she unlocked her front door. "You don't have to take care of me. I'm a grown-up."

"That's right, you are. Now let me inside. It's baltic out here."

"You are such a baby. It's not that cold."

I cocked a brow but held my tongue because she let me inside. "Where's the loo?" I asked, shrugging out of my coat.

"Don't get comfortable. Leave the jacket on, Taylor."

"Afraid you'll get the wrong idea and want to take me to bed?"

"You are delusional."

"You know, it's perfectly fine to want your husband in the biblical sense, lass."

A soft gasp tore Becca's gaze from mine. I

followed her focus to where Scarlett stood, eyes wide, mouth agape, a tray of cupcakes tilting precariously in her hold.

"Husband?"

"Aye." I wrapped one arm around Becca and pulled her close. "You got yourself a new brother-in-law."

Scarlett's tray of fairy cakes tipped, the pastel-decorated treats falling to the floor in a multicolored splat.

"Shit, you couldn't have let me ease her into it?" Becca pulled free of my hold and rushed to her sister to help her clean up.

"You got married?" she hissed. "To him?"

"I'm right here. I can hear you, you know."

"I did it for a reason," I grumbled. "I'll explain everything after he leaves."

"It's better she find out now rather than read it on the news tonight after the auction anyway. I don't know why you're cross with me."

Her gaze could have set me on fire if she'd had the power. "I was going to tell her before that. Just not with you in the room, taking up every available ounce of space."

I leaned against the table and smirked. "From where I'm standing, there's plenty of space in this house."

"I think she means in her head."

"Scarlett, that's not helpful. His ego is already so big I don't know how he fit through the door."

I excused myself to use the toilet, and when I returned, the Barnes sisters were still chattering about Becca's decision. I couldn't really add anything beneficial to the conversation, so I planted a kiss on my bride's cheek and said, "As lovely as this has been, I'll be off. I hope you're planning to wear something sexy tonight, wife. It's our wedding night, after all. I plan to show you off to my mates and make a fucking splash with our news. *Meet-Cupid* won't know what hit 'em."

Becca swallowed hard, her face going a touch pale.

"Don't worry, lass. This is a good thing. You'll see. Being the wife of Taylor Savage isn't the worst thing that could happen to you."

"Oh, no? Then what is?"

I winked. "Never being mine at all."

She laughed nervously, and I knew exactly why. Because this arrangement was temporary. Fleeting. And if I didn't pull back on the flirty banter, it would end up being dangerous to both of us.

But after I was back in my car and headed toward the ferry terminal, the worry about falling for Becca was eclipsed by a multitude of emails from my agent, from Eva, the team's publicist, and from Trick Huston. Offers for off-season stints on reality dating shows, requirements from

Meet-Cupid, and then my teammate needing my help with his own date.

No matter how attracted to Becca Barnes I was, falling in love wasn't an option. She was getting me out of years of obligation to life as an eligible bachelor in the public eye. I was helping her with her kitchen. It was a win-win. And if one thing was for certain, I loved to win.

8

BECCA

The morning after the charity event was like any other morning. Get up at the crack of dawn, go for a run to get my blood flowing, then caffeinate, hydrate, and shower. That was the plan. Except, of course, Taylor had publicly introduced me as his wife to his entire team and some of the richest people in Seattle last night. It felt like everyone was watching me as I passed. Let them watch.

Just because I was married to the bad boy Scot with a heart of gold, as he was now named, that didn't mean I had to change a damn thing. Except as my feet pounded the pavement on the street where I lived, the last few yards of my run turning to a cool down, my heart rate did anything but slow. Taylor Savage stood on my front porch, a large duffel bag in his hands and a shit-eating grin on his stupid handsome face.

"What are you doing here?"

Eyes widening, he scoffed. "Well now, hen, is that any way to speak to your husband? Your one and only. The love of your life."

"Try bane of my existence. Why are you here, Taylor?"

"I'm moving in. It was part of our arrangement, remember?"

"No. You were buying a house for us to live in. You never said anything about us moving into this house. My sister lives here too."

"I would get us a house, but the market is wild these days. Why stress over it when you have a perfectly good place ready for us?" He waggled his eyebrows. "It can be our little love nest."

"You said you already had one in the works."

His gaze dropped to his feet for just a second. "Aye, I did. And that was true. But someone else swooped in and made a better offer. The wanker."

"So go home to Seattle until you find a different place."

He shook his head. "No can do, I'm afraid. The press is already lurking outside my building. They'll know something's up if you aren't with me. The last thing I need is another relationship scandal. After the whole . . . Katerina debacle, my reputation could use a little polishing."

I bit back a flash of jealousy at the mention of

the supermodel he'd dated, the one who ended up being married to a high-powered businessman. The tabloids had a field day with the very public fight that ended with Taylor spending a night in jail.

"So I'm the polish? Your fake wife?"

"There's nothing fake about this, Tink. You married me."

"But it's just an arrangement. You need to remember that."

"An arrangement that's as real as anything. Don't worry. I'm not after making you fall in love with me. I know that's not on the table for us. We made that clear our first go round."

Something in my chest tightened, a dull throb that twisted and turned into a stabbing pain. Why? He was right. We'd gone out more than once, which had been a disaster, but the final time was the nail in our coffin. When he'd tried so hard to convince me that being at a wedding with another woman wasn't a big deal. But he wanted to move in . . . here? The problem between us had nothing to do with attraction and everything to do with the fact that he was arrogant, overconfident, and a player.

"Taylor, I don't think it's a good idea. Scarlett—"

"I'm not asking her to leave. I just . . . we have to make this work. You agreed."

"What do you think we need to do to make

this work?" I asked, staring at him with my heart in my throat. "We're certainly not sleeping together."

"Oh, lass, you wound me. Am I that easy to read?"

"Yeah. You're exactly that. I remember very clearly just how easy you were. I bet you've never spent a single night alone you didn't want to."

Something like hurt flashed across his face. "You really think I'm that terrible?"

"You haven't proven anything different. Why wouldn't I?"

His jaw set. "Fine. That doesn't change the fact that you married me and made an agreement with me."

"You're right. I did. Fine. But you can sleep on the couch."

I saw the argument in his eyes. He wanted so much to tell me exactly what he thought of sleeping on the sofa. Instead of saying another word, he gave a curt nod and hitched his bag over his shoulder. "Let me inside, then, Tink. I'm fucking starved and need a shower."

"Charming."

"You would too if you'd come all the way from practice with every possession packed."

"This isn't every possession you have. There's no way."

"No, but it is all my clothes and everything important."

"What did you do with the rest of your stuff?"

He shrugged. "I gave it to Petrov."

"Excuse me?"

"He needed a place to live anyway. Fucking Eva told him his bachelor pad was pathetic. He decided he needed to find a new place and mine just so happened to be available since I'm a married man and all."

"I see. That's very generous of you."

The way he winked at me had my belly clenching. "I'm nothing if not a humanitarian, lass. Why else would you have fallen desperately in love with me when we first met?"

I snorted. I couldn't help myself. "Yeah, because nothing says love like a trip to the emergency room and anaphylaxis."

"I couldn't help it you tried to kill me. You found my one weakness."

"Cardamom. So unsuspecting and delicious."

"I'll pass on that. Deadly and devious, more like. That wee spice has nearly ruined my day more than once."

"Death does seem to put a damper on one's day."

"It won't kill me, you know."

"What?"

"Nae. It just makes my lips all puffy and my throat itch."

"But . . . you . . . EpiPen . . ."

"I keep it in case the reaction gets severe."

"So we didn't need to go to the hospital that night?"

He grinned, and I wanted to throttle him. "No, but you were so adorably concerned. If you recall, there was no changing your mind. You drove like a bat out of hell."

"So what did they do to you at the hospital?"

"Gave me a strong dose of Benadryl."

Jesus, this man was infuriating. "Why didn't you tell me?"

"Would you really have listened? I don't think so. You had it in your mind that you'd killed me. How on earth were you going to explain that one to your sister?"

I winced. It had flashed in my mind more than once on the drive to the hospital that I was going to have to explain the death of my brother-in-law's star player.

"Right, then. Glad to have that out of the way. Anything else you're allergic to? I should take notes."

"Why, so you can kill me?"

"Maybe."

"Sadly for you, cardamom is my only weak point. Nothing else can take me down." He shifted from foot to foot, his gaze trailing up the stairs. "So, about that shower?"

I rolled my eyes and said, "Top of the stairs, first door on the right."

Fifteen minutes later, he still hadn't come

downstairs, and I was getting antsy. What was he doing up there? Investigating my closet? Stealing my panties? Rolling around in my sheets so I'd have to smell him when I went to bed? It seemed fitting he'd be trying to mark his territory. Freaking alpha male athletes.

I tromped up the stairs, calling his name, but he didn't answer. When I knocked open the bathroom door, there was only silence. "Taylor?"

The shower wasn't running. The light wasn't on either. Oh, this man. Where the hell was he?

Sure enough, I found his bag settled smack dab in the middle of my bed, his clothes discarded on my floor in a trail into my adjoining bathroom. The shower was running, steam creeping out of the open door, and the burly tattooed Scot was singing at full volume. Was that... "Wrecking Ball" by Miley Cyrus?

As quickly as I could, I grabbed my clothes out of my drawer, needing my own shower before my day really got started. I sure as shit wasn't going to join him. I'd just have to use Scarlett's bathroom this morning. The excuse of having an errant husband taking up space in mine was solid enough.

"Oh, Tink, if you'd wanted to join me, all you had to do was ask."

His rumbled brogue had tingles racing up my spine. I swear to God, if he weren't so frustrating, he'd be deadly to my panties. Especially after I turned around and caught sight of him bare-chested and wearing nothing but my pale pink towel around his . . . bits. "I had no intention of joining you. I'm here to get my clothes since *someone* decided to ignore my instructions. Don't know your right from your left, Taylor? Is that something they don't teach in Scotland?"

"I know exactly where I belong. In your room. You're my wife."

"In name only. That means my space is off limits."

"I wasnae going to intrude on Scarlett's privacy. She could have had personal items in there."

I huffed. The nerve of this man. "*I* have personal items in there!" I gestured to the bathroom.

A wicked smirk twisted his lips. "Oh, I know. I found them."

My cheeks heated. Them. He'd found them. "What exactly?"

"Your . . . toys. You left one out on the counter. It's quite large. I didn't think you'd be into butt stuff. Anal beads are a much more advanced kink than I expected from someone like you."

I laughed out loud. "Anal beads? What are you talking about?"

"Your anal beads are sitting right there next to

the sink. Do they vibrate or something? You forgot to plug them in to charge."

Storming into the bathroom, I rolled my eyes as I grabbed what he mistook for anal beads. "This is a curling wand. It doesn't go up my butt."

"Are you sure? It looks like something you'd stick up your bum."

"No, Taylor. It's for my hair. God. What are you into that you'd even think that was possible?"

His laugh told me everything I needed to know. He'd been fucking with me.

"Put some clothes on. I'm going to take my shower now. When I get out, I expect you to be nowhere near this room. Got it?"

"Aye, my wee darling. I'll get out of your hair. But . . . if you ever want me to teach you about the things I'm into . . ."

"Get the fuck out of my room."

This was going to be impossible.

TAYLOR

Oh, this was going to be a bloody good time.

Becca was so easy to rile up. All I had to do was smirk in her general direction, and she was ready for a fight. I dressed while she turned on the shower, the thought of her naked in the bathroom doing things to my body she would be so cross about. I couldn't help it. She was so feisty and adorable. And cardamom aside, her lips were the most kissable things I'd ever seen. I still thought about that kiss we'd shared. The only time she let me bring our bodies together. Not that I hadn't wanted to.

If I hadn't fucked it all up, she'd be mine right now in every way, not just this daft marriage of convenience I'd convinced myself was necessary. I was such a stupid git. I could've bought my way out of the contract. Could have done anything else to get out of it. Instead, I latched on to the one idea I somehow thought would be easiest.

My phone buzzed in my pocket, a text from Trick.

Trick: How's the wife? She take kindly to you showing up with all your shit?

Me: No is too gentle a word.

Trick: Did she cut your cock off with a kitchen knife yet?

I cupped my junk instinctively.

Me: No. Not yet.

Trick: Not yet. Smart man. You know it's coming.

Me: She'll come around.

Trick: Are you sure you want to go through with this? You can just get a quickie divorce. She won't care.

Me: It's already all over the news. Everyone knows.

Trick: So?

I didn't want to admit to him how important it was to me to save face. Maybe I was being stubborn, but I didn't want to fail at this. I'd honor my commitment to her. Help her get her kitchen up and running. Then we'd part as friends. It was a perfect plan.

Trick: Are you bringing her to Big Deck's engagement party?

Me: I haven't asked her yet.

Honestly, I'd just assumed she'd be there. As soon as Ethan had proposed, Becca and Scarlett swooped in and started planning the event. It would be small but a fun night if they had anything to say about it.

"Oh. It's you." Scarlett stood in the kitchen as I walked inside, tucking my phone away.

"It's me."

"What..."

"I'm moving in. I hope you don't mind. The wife and I need to be together. You know, for appearances."

Scarlett frowned, then took her bottom lip between her teeth. "Well, that makes this a little easier, then."

"Makes what easier?" Becca said, bounding down the stairs. Her face was freshly scrubbed, free of makeup, and her cheeks were a bright pink. I loved how her eyes sparkled and the spray of freckles across the bridge of her nose was visible.

"I'm moving out."

"What?" The hurt in Becca's voice had me wishing I could pull her in for an embrace. Wait, no. I didn't want to hug my wife. I had no interest in this being more than what it was. Us helping each other.

"I just need to spend some time on my own. You making this choice with Taylor, marrying him like you did, showed me exactly why. I'm missing out on too much being so sheltered here. I need to live a little."

"Scar—"

"I'm not trying to upset you, but it's the truth. You and Clara protected me from everything. It's time for me to see more of the world. I can't stay safe in our little bakery bubble all the time. So this is the perfect opportunity."

"Where are you going?"

She shrugged. "I'm leasing the apartment above the bakery. I set it up last week. I'm moving in two days."

Becca let out a little squeak of protest. "Two days? You've known about this for a week?"

Scarlett nodded. "It's not like I could tell you. Not when you were off getting married without talking to me. Now the two of you can have the house to yourselves."

I didn't mind that at all, aside from the fact that it clearly hurt Becca to know her sister was leaving. I might've fucked up a lot more than I thought by springing this on Tink.

They went quiet, both of them looking away, refusing to talk about the elephant in the room . . . me.

"Oh, look . . . cinnamon buns. I love cinnamon."

I reached for one, and Becca let out a soft huff. "Too bad they're not cardamom."

9

BECCA

I couldn't get over the sight of Taylor standing nearly naked in the window as he sipped his coffee and stared out at the backyard. In fact, I couldn't stop looking at him from my vantage point out in the gazebo. For the last two months, he just walked around shirtless all damn day. What was I supposed to do with that? My battery-operated boyfriend was definitely earning his keep because of the man.

I pressed my feet more firmly into the thick padding of the yoga mat as I forced myself to focus on my breathing, the feel of the breeze blowing across my skin, anything but the handsome man I'd married who was currently grinning at me and ... flexing.

The beautiful bastard.

Turning around, I began my sun salutation cycle. Normally I faced the house because that was where the sunshine beamed at this time of day, but something about my audience made me think facing away would be more effective.

I dipped down into a forward fold, then came up to chair pose before dropping fully to another forward bend and placing my palms on the mat. The sound of the back door sliding open caught my ear, but I didn't stop. I stepped back into plank pose, then lowered myself to the mat before lifting my chest and taking a beat in cobra. I loved the way this stretched my chest and throat, my lower spine and belly. Then on my next exhale, I lifted my hips into downward-facing dog. It used to be my least favorite, but now, all the tension in my shoulders seeped into the ground.

"Bloody fucking Christ, lass. Are you determined to give me blue balls all damned day? I have to do a school talk this afternoon, but now all I'll be able to see is your perfect fucking arse up in the air begging me to take a bite out of it."

"That sounds a lot like a you problem, Taylor. I'm just exercising."

I stepped one foot forward and brought myself into warrior pose, not allowing myself to look at him.

"Is that what you call it?"

"What would you say it is?"

I risked a glance over my shoulder. Freaking bad boy in low-slung sweats and a black tank. At least he covered all that toned muscle before he came outside. But why did part of me wish he hadn't?

He grinned at me as he sipped his coffee.

"I'd call it a fucking tease."

"I'm supposed to believe that you looking like . . . that isn't your attempt to tease me too?"

One brow lifted as he brought the mug to his lips, the tattoos on his arm shifting with the motion. "Is that your way of telling me you want me, Tink? We are married now, after all. There's no shame in wanting your husband to rail you into next week."

"You're really confident that you know how to please me."

But if I was being honest, the idea of him having his way with me had always been appealing. It was the rest of him I had issues with. The way he had begun to make me feel when we first met, the way he scared me. He looked at me on that first date like I was the one for him. That wasn't something I believed in. This? The business deal that our marriage was made sense to me. We helped each other achieve a common goal. It was easy. We didn't have to fall in love and go through all the heartache that would inevitably follow. All we needed to do was stay together for one year. Ten more months.

"Do you have your dress for the gala tonight?" he called, knocking back the rest of his coffee as soon as he finished speaking.

Another gala. I was drowning in galas.

"Why? Do you need to give your approval?"

"I just want to make sure I choose the right tie to go with whatever color you're wearing. What good is being married if we don't look the part?"

"It's champagne colored."

"I've got just the thing. Do you want to try it on for me before we get ready? Maybe let me help you with your lingerie?"

I went back into downward-facing dog, and he groaned. "I wasn't planning on wearing anything under it."

"Jesus fucking Christ."

"If you have a problem with that, maybe you shouldn't go with me."

"I'm going to be attached to your side the whole night. Spinning you around the dance floor and making sure every single bloke there knows you're mine."

God, sometimes he was so damn sexy. Deadly to my resolve. Exactly my type of bad boy.

And I'd just have to keep myself from falling for his special brand of charm. The one that made my panties wet and my vagina beg for attention. She wanted to know exactly what all those rolling Rs did for the Scotsman's tongue.

The shameless slut.

"Okay, I'm here. I'm dressed and ready to pretend I like you."

Taylor chuckled. His smirk was cocky and infuriating all at the same time.

"It shouldn't be hard to pretend when it's not far from the truth, lass. Especially when you look like that." His gaze raked my form, taking in every inch of the sparkling champagne-colored gown I wore. It fit like a glove and showcased my curves in a way I would have once been told was indecent.

"That's what you think. It couldn't be further from the truth."

"Oh, you wound me. You know, for a tiny wee thing, you certainly are vicious."

"You must bring it out in me. In fact, I made you some cupcakes. Would you care to try them? They're your favorite." His eyes widened with excitement before he narrowed them. "Cardamom."

He shook his head, a serious frown marring his brow. "You wouldn't try to kill me. Not for real."

"You already told me it won't kill you. I just like to see you squirm."

"You know, my wee wife, has it ever crossed your mind that it might not be hate you feel for me?"

"It did the first time we went out together."

"And the second?"

I shook my head. "After that, I quickly realized the error of my ways."

He let out a groan I could only call sexy and cupped himself. "God, but she's trying to rile me up before sending me out to the firing squad."

"I'm not trying to do anything, Taylor."

"That's what you say. But you're still managing perfectly well."

I needed to change the subject. I couldn't deal with him.

"What about you? Is that what you're wearing? How come I have to dress in black tie, and you get to just sit there looking like"—I waved up and down his body—"that."

He was dressed in black slacks and a white button-down, complete with the sleeves rolled up to the forearm. Did he know I was a slut for hot forearms? Probably not. Or maybe the asshole did. I wouldn't put it past him to use his body against me.

"I'm not quite ready yet. I was actually hoping you'd give me a little help."

"Help with what?"

"Well, I've never been good at tying these things. Do you think maybe you could give it a go?"

The innocence in his voice had my whole body humming. That one gesture of vulnerability reminded me of the man I'd fallen hard for on our first date. Even if he'd revealed himself to be nothing like that in reality.

"I don't understand why men insist on wearing this stuff."

He laughed. "Do you have a problem with formal wear? How could that possibly offend you?"

"I don't have a problem with it. Aside from how hot it is."

"As in sexy?"

"Maybe."

"What else could you possibly mean?"

"Well, hot as in actually warm."

"Oh, my darlin wee lass"—he lowered his voice—"that's why we take it off as soon as we get home."

I gulped, not really wanting to picture him taking anything off. We might have been married, but that was as far as it went between us—for good reason. The last thing I wanted was to fall for him, because I knew exactly where I'd end up if I did. Alone.

"Who hurt you, hen?"

"What?"

"I saw the way your eyes dimmed. Something flashed across your face clear as day, and it wasn't because of my joke about undressing. Someone hurt you. Who was it?"

I let my guard down and made the mistake of letting a man see my vulnerable pieces. Securing my mask, I pasted a bright smile on my face.

"Who hasn't?"

"You might think I'm after hurting you, too, but you couldn't be more wrong."

As I snatched the bow tie from his hands, I rose onto my tiptoes so I could make sure the silk was perfectly nestled under his collar. I forced my gaze to remain on his throat rather than let myself look at the mouth he'd no doubt be smirking with.

"Do you think you'll ever forgive me, hen?"

"For what? There's nothing to forgive."

"Clearly there is. I mucked everything up bad enough to make you cross with me. To make you drop me the way you have."

"I didn't drop you. We weren't good together."

"Of course we were. Lass, we were fire. We just never got a chance to burn."

I scoffed. "Just stop. Pretty words aren't gonna get you anywhere."

"They're not pretty, but they are true."

His throat bobbed as he swallowed and waited for my response.

I kept my focus on the silk between my

fingers as I continued tying the bow. "I don't know how to be *this* with you. To be the woman in your life."

"Forgive me for saying this because it might seem obvious, but I think the only way you do it is exactly what you're doing right now."

I put the finishing touches on the tie and then turned away from him. But he caught me by the elbow and pulled me against his body.

"You don't get to run off, hen. We have to have a conversation about where we stand and where we're headed, and I'm not letting you hide just because it's hard. The two of us have a lot to talk about."

"No, we don't. We actually have very little to discuss. I'm going with you to this stupid party, coming home, and we're going to our separate rooms, and we're not going—"

"I think you know that's a lie."

"It's not." My protest sounded hollow even to my own ears. It was weak.

"You want me just like I want you."

"I don't . . . I can't . . . just because you're attractive . . ." I hated the way I was a spluttering mess under his attention.

"Oh, you do think I'm handsome?"

The scoff I released was neither ladylike nor classy. "Of course I do. I have eyes."

The asshole smirked and then chuckled. "I'm glad you finally admitted it to yourself."

"If you don't shut up, I'm gonna shut you up."

"I'd like to see you try."

"Don't tempt me."

Sighing, I rolled my eyes. "You are the most infuriating thing, but that doesn't stop me from wanting to kiss you."

"You can't."

"I can. All you have to do is say the word."

We locked eyes for a few heartbeats. His intense stare had me clenching my thighs together, hoping for a way to distract myself from those tempting lips. I couldn't stop imagining more.

"Do you really not want to take advantage of this situation we've found ourselves in?"

"What are you talking about?"

His palms slid around my waist, and I didn't stop him. "Well, two consenting adults . . . consenting. Doesn't it seem the slightest bit odd if we don't take advantage? We could"—he gave a lascivious waggle of his brows—"you know."

"Are you actually suggesting we—"

"Until neither of us can walk straight? Yes. Yes, I am."

Was it hot in here? Why was my throat so tight? I had to have heard him wrong because there was no way he just suggested we have sex.

"Taylor, are you high?" I backed out of his hold, staying close enough he could grab me again if he wanted to.

"No. I think it's a way to make the best out of our predicament."

"Predicament? This is not a predicament. This is an arrangement we made together."

He gave me a pleading look. "Aye, it is, but it's also an arrangement that has left me in a serious state over the last two months."

What did he mean by a serious state? Then it hit me. The man was horny, and he seemed to think I was fair game simply because I'd married him. "Oh," I said, trying to wrap my brain around this new wrinkle in our agreement. "So you and I . . . How would that even work?"

He smirked. "Well, first you get naked, and second—"

"I understand how it works." I wasn't a virgin like my sister.

"It doesn't have to change anything between us, but I think we'd both benefit if we, you know . . . fuck now and then."

Of course he did. Cocky fucker. "So you to get off and I get what? An STI?"

The eye roll he gave me said he was not amused. "I'm not going to give you an STI. I don't know how you think I could."

"I've checked out your dating profile on *Meet-Cupid*."

"Oh, you mean the one I never use?"

"The one you *say* you never use."

"The only person I dated on that app was you."

"We never dated on that app."

"No, but you were on it, weren't you?"

"At my sister's request, yes."

"And I did the same at the team's request. You can't hold that against me."

I sighed deeply. He was right. I couldn't hold it against him. Not if I wanted to avoid being a hypocrite of epic proportions. "This is exhausting."

"What is?"

"Fighting with you all the time. You can't tell me you actually enjoy it."

"No, I don't. I don't want to fight with you. Same as I don't want to have to continue a life of celibacy."

"Well, the two of us are not going there. So don't get your hopes up."

"Is being with me so bad?"

"Being with you is dangerous."

"What makes it dangerous?"

"Well, you're you."

"I'm what?"

"You're cocky and flirty and . . ."

"It's all right. You can say it. I'm dead sexy."

I laughed despite myself. "Yes, you're sexy."

"I knew you liked me."

Crossing my arms over my chest, I bit my lip. "I'm not ready to risk myself with you."

"I don't know why you think I'm such a risk."

"Taylor, I've fallen for men like you before, and it doesn't end well for me."

"I'm not asking you to fall for me."

"I know. You're asking me to like you. To fall into bed with you. To help you get some release. I get it. I do."

"Get what?"

"That you need someone to work out all this testosterone with." I hated the words even as they left my lips. "You have my blessing."

"What do you mean?"

"I mean, go find yourself some other woman to bang. Someone who can do casual. It's not me. It wouldn't be fair to you or to me."

"That's not part of our arrangement. We said no one else."

"That was before you started trying to seduce me."

His eyes narrowed as that sharp jaw clenched. "And what if I don't want some other woman?"

"Then I guess you better stock up on lotion and Kleenex, buddy. Because this isn't a line we can cross."

"Fine. Maybe it's better if we both find someone else."

"Sure, whatever."

Why did that hurt? It wasn't supposed to. I had a plan. An agreement. I would just wait out my year. Quietly divorce him, and look back on my time. God, how had I ended up a plot line straight out of a regency romance? And why did I feel like my heart was going to end up broken, just like the heroines in those books, if I let him get any closer to me?

10

TAYLOR

"So how's married life, Savage? You got any pearls of wisdom for us bachelors?" Trick asked as we warmed up on the ice.

He passed me the puck, a smirk curling up his lips.

"Better than spending my nights trolling bars. I don't miss that. I go home to the most beautiful woman I've ever seen. Can't complain, now, can I?"

I took my shot, sneaking the puck past him and straight to Byrne.

"And the boss really doesn't have any issues with you fucking his sister-in-law?"

Trick twisted away from where Byrne had him blocked and snagged the puck as the big Brit cursed under his breath.

"That's not really his business, is it? I can spend my time with whoever I want. Maverick Wilde doesn't scare me. He barely knows anything about hockey and spends most of his time with his hands—"

The ice was deathly quiet as my words died on my tongue because standing there, watching me with an amused smirk on his lips, was the man himself. He wore a dark cowboy hat, a pair of jeans, and I'm sure if I could see past the boards, a pair of boots. He didn't look one bit like a team owner should. This guy didn't fit in, and the way he ran our team only drove that idea home.

"Go on, Savage. Keep goin'. Don't hold back. Where do I keep my hands?"

Byrne snorted, and I shot him a look that said he'd be paying for that later.

"Very wisely on your money, Mr. Wilde."

He jutted his chin toward the team. "Good answer. Keep practicing. I'm not here, got it?"

Trick took that as his opportunity to get one over, and he shot the puck past me. It made it into the goal before Petrov could even blink.

"Gotta think fast, Savage."

If I didn't like Trick so much, I'd shove him into the boards for that. Actually, maybe I would do it anyway. But as I geared up to go after him, Maverick spoke again.

"We're gonna need a sit down after practice is over. I'll be waiting for you in my office."

I couldn't deny the way those words made my gut churn. I wasn't interested in dealing with a pushy team owner or a protective older brother type, but I had a feeling I'd be getting both.

"Savage is in trouble," Trick taunted.

"And Trick is about to have his ass handed to him," I muttered.

I pummeled him when all was said and done. My team won the scrimmage, and he had to lick his wounds in front of everyone. It was bloody fantastic. But now I had to face the music. Maverick was waiting on me, and I knew fuck all of what he was going to say.

Pulling my shirt over my head, I tucked my phone into my pocket and headed to the owner's office. The previous Mr. Wilde hadn't been involved at all. He'd been a silent partner, leaving the management of the team to the manager. I think I liked that better.

With a sharp knock on the door, I cleared my throat and waited to hear him invite me inside. It took all of two seconds for him to call out, "Come on in, Taylor."

Much to my surprise, I didn't find the stern, protective man I was expecting. Maverick Wilde sat behind his desk, boots resting on the polished wood with a glass of what looked like whiskey in his hand.

"Have a seat. I poured you one already."

"What's this all about?"

Why did I feel like I was in danger of being capped by the cowboy Mafia? Was there a cowboy Mafia? Probably. If there was, he was in it.

"I just want to talk."

Yep, cowboy Mafia. Fuck.

"If you're gonna be my brother-in-law, I figured we needed some time to get to know each other. Officially."

"Are you here to tell me how you'll kill me if I hurt her?"

He smirked and took a sip of whiskey. "Sort of."

"Look, I don't intend to do anything to hurt Becca."

"Good, because I know how it goes with athletes. You marry the girl, but then all that time on the road gets lonely, and you're only a man. You just need relief. What she doesn't know won't hurt her, and so on." He leveled his stare on me. "That's not gonna happen here, is it?"

I took the glass of amber liquid and brought it to my lips. The vanilla and smoke flavor burst on my tongue, making me fight the urge to cough. "No. I'm not a cheater. Never have been."

"That's not what your history says."

"I. Don't. Cheat. Not on anyone, and never on Becca."

"Good, because I love her sister somethin' fierce, and if anything happened to that girl, my wife would be just as heartbroken."

I could see it in his eyes. He was serious.

"Anything that happens between Becca and me will only happen if she wants it to."

He lifted his glass in a cheers gesture. "Then I guess, welcome to the family, Savage."

"Thank you, sir."

I didn't know what else to say. It wasn't like I could explain that we'd started this farce out knowing it had an end date. So, I drank my whiskey down and then stood. "If there's nothing else, I have a long commute home, and my wife is waiting on me."

With a curt nod, he turned his attention to the computer on his desk. "Tell her to set up supper at our place, will ya? Quinn needs to meet her new uncle."

"Supper?"

"Yeah. That's how we do it around these parts, Savage. You get together with the in-laws. I promised Clara I'd help her be closer with her sisters. Now you're attached to one of them. That means you come with her."

Unease settled itself in my throat, a ball of worry so big I couldn't get words out. So I nodded instead before leaving. Becca had been avoiding the team and everything connected to it since the auction. I knew why. She didn't want to explain it all to Clara.

My wife hadn't explained much of her background, but I'd gathered enough through simply listening. Her parents died young, and Clara took on the role of caregiver.

She hadn't seen her elder sister since right after we were married.

I pulled out my phone and sent her a quick text as I returned to the locker room to collect the rest of my stuff.

Me: It's time to stop avoiding your family, Tink.

Tink: You're not the boss of me.

I chuckled under my breath. I could hear the petulance from a mile away.

Me: Yeah, well, my boss is asking for a family dinner with us, so I'd say if you don't want things to be awkward as arse, you have to talk to Clara.

Tink: Shit.

Me: I know. It's going to be hard to keep your hands off me, but you'll do your best when we go over there.

Tink: Ha.

Me: I'll be home in about an hour. Perhaps we should practice not hating each other.

Tink: I don't like to set myself up for failure.

Oh, that was a wicked blow.

Me: It won't be hard for me. I must be a better actor than you.

Tink: Don't be proud you're a better liar than I am. That's not a skill you should flaunt.

I wondered how she'd feel about me putting her over my knee and spanking the insolence out of her. Probably better not to try. I wanted to have children eventually, and I wouldn't be able to do that if she crushed my bollocks in her hands.

11

BECCA

It wasn't that I didn't like hockey, I had just never been into any kind of sport. But tonight, I had to show up for my husband. I was obligated to do this for Taylor; truthfully, I had no problem with it. It turned out that nearly everything he participated in was some form of charity. Funding for the new library? Taylor Savage was involved. After-school programs? You guessed it. Taylor Savage was there. He seemed to have a soft spot for underprivileged children and education, and God help me, I was having a really hard time holding on to my dislike of him. Especially given how charming he'd been at dinner with my family.

Sure, he was cocky and overconfident, but I wondered if that was all part of the front. If the

Taylor Savage the public saw in interviews with NHL blogs or on morning news shows was really the same guy as the man who'd inserted himself into my life. I had a sneaking suspicion it wasn't.

"What are you wearing?" he asked as he stood in the doorway of my bedroom.

I turned around and grinned at him. "You don't like it?" I knew what all the WAGs did. They wore their guy's jersey. It wasn't a question. I'd agreed to come to this function, which happened to be a teddy bear toss game for St. Jude Medical Center, so I was going to look the part.

"You're wearing my number," he said, a possessive note in his voice I liked way too much.

"So? I'm your wife. Don't you think it would look a little weird if I didn't?"

"Perhaps. I just didn't realize you even knew my number."

I glanced over my shoulder at myself in the mirror. Savage was written across my back, 19 loud and proud underneath. The navy blue and teal jersey complimented my eyes, if I did say so myself. "Taylor, I'm not that uninvested. Of course I know your number. And I know what position you play. And I know your stats are really really—"

"How many goals did I make this season?"

I rattled off the number like it was my own name.

His brows rose. "Impressive. How many assists?"

I told him that number too.

"You really are paying attention."

"Yes. What kind of wife would I be if I didn't support my husband? I even know how many times you've been in the penalty box. You're a naughty boy, Taylor Savage."

"You knew that before you married me."

"I did. But if you want, I can change. Wear one of the other guys' jerseys, maybe? I'm sure I could call Elles. She has a spare number 41 lying around—"

"Don't you fucking dare."

"That's what I thought." I couldn't stop my laugh. They were all possessive cavemen when it came down to it. Even if Taylor and I were married in name only.

"I have to go. Do you want to come with me? You can wait in the owner's box. No one else is in there since Mav and Clara went back to Montana."

"Sure. Scarlett was going to meet me later, but it seems silly for us to take two cars."

"Aye, that it does."

"Unless you're planning to stay in Seattle tonight." Why did part of me hate that idea?

"No, I belong here with you. Unless you . . . unless you don't want me to come back."

I wanted him to come back so much more

than I should. As hard as I tried not to, somehow I'd grown accustomed to my husband. I liked seeing his stupid face every morning, listening to him singing in the shower—off key and very loud. I thought I might actually want to be friends with him. What the heck was that about?

Once the two of us had cleared the air and set some real ground rules about what we could and couldn't do—no kissing, touching, seduction, and definitely no sex—my rigidness had eased up quite a bit and became more of a general caution. Our problem had never been that I didn't like Taylor. The problem was that he was way more my type than I wanted to admit, and I wasn't ready for him. He could ruin me if he wanted to. Allowing that wasn't on my list of things to do.

"You look good," he said with a grin. "In my number."

I didn't know how to respond. So instead I simply smiled and said, "Thank you. I do try."

"It's not something you have to try for. You always look good, hen."

I wondered if this glimpse of the sweet guy he was giving me—so similar to the man from our first date—was the real him one more time. Why did he feel like he had to hide behind a mask of machismo to think it made him more attractive? Because to me, it was the complete opposite. That cocksure attitude turned me off faster than anything else he could have done.

We drove together to the arena, and I was in awe as we walked through the players' entrance.

"You can't seriously tell me you've never been to a game. Your sister's the owner."

"I've seen them on TV and clips online but I've never been."

"You don't like hockey?"

"I don't know the rules."

"And you like to play by the rules, don't you?"

"Yes. Rules keep things organized and fair. Can keep people from getting hurt."

"Well, you want me to explain them to you now?"

"Do you want to?"

"I don't mind." He threaded our fingers as we walked through winding corridors in the most secret parts of the arena.

"Then yes, please, explain."

He detailed the rules of the game in a way I could mostly understand, but I really needed to see him in action before it would all sink in.

"So that's your job? Are you good at it?"

"I wouldn't be here if I wasn't."

"Do you like it?"

"Do I like what?"

"Playing defense?"

"Aye, I like it. Of course I do. I wouldn't have left everything behind so I could chase this dream if I didn't."

"And what about . . ." I stumbled on my words, a little embarrassment creeping up.

"Are you blushing, hen?"

Swallowing back my nerves, I blurted, "I heard somewhere that hockey players often lose their teeth and wear fake ones." I couldn't help myself. I chuckled when he opened his mouth and tapped on his teeth.

"Sometimes, yes, that happens. These are mine. All of them, I assure you."

"Are any of the guys missing teeth?"

"A few."

"Which ones?"

"Do you really want to know?"

I nodded. "Absolutely."

"Reuben is missing a couple. His top two fronts got knocked out when he was in primary school right after the adult ones had just grown in. He wears false ones now. You'll see if you catch him smiling after the game before he puts them back in."

"It seems like such a dangerous sport."

"Oh, it's only a wee bit dangerous."

"Well, I don't know many sports where you regularly get your teeth knocked out—except for rugby."

"Rugby is pretty vicious. Not much padding."

"Did you ever play it in Scotland?"

"I did. It was kind of a rite of passage for my family. But I fell in love with hockey, much to my family's disappointment. I'm very good at disappointing them."

I bristled, remembering that the last time we'd spoken about his family, it hadn't gone well. He hadn't brought them up since then. "Did you tell your mom?"

"Tell her what?"

"That we got married."

"Not yet. I was hoping perhaps to avoid them finding out before . . . you know . . . we meet the end of the road together."

"I suppose them being all the way in Scotland makes that a little more likely."

"Maybe."

"Don't you think they're going to see it if they keep track of you at all?"

His jaw clenched. "Probably stands to reason they will."

"I guess that's one bonus to not having parents. I don't have to face them when I do dumb stuff."

"Would you really call it dumb?" Something about the way he said that made my heart twist.

"What? I . . ." I had to think about that for a moment. "Not really. We're grown-ups. We're allowed to make decisions like this."

He smiled. "And my decision to marry the prettiest girl I've ever seen is still one I stand by."

That made my belly flip. He really could be charming when he wanted to. After dropping me off at the owner's box, he left me with a soft kiss on the cheek and flicked his gaze over to where the manager was watching. Flanked by none other than the team's PR manager, who immediately came over to me.

"Well, it looks like you two are finally settling into married life. How's he doing?"

"I think he's fine."

"You never know with Savage. He's kind of a wild card, and with everything going on back home..."

"Everything?"

"Yes. His grandfather is barely hanging on now. Everything." She acted like I should know all the details. And of course I should. I was his wife.

"Oh, right. That everything. Sorry, there's a lot to keep track of with hockey and"—I laughed nervously—"everything."

Taylor's grandfather was dying, and he hadn't even told me.

"I assume the two of you will be heading to Scotland after the season and—"

"Scotland?" I choked on the word.

"Just let me know if you need help arranging the travel. I know a travel agent. She's fantastic. She'll get you set up so you won't have any trouble booking flights to Scotland."

"I'll check with him. I think he might be doing that on his own."

"Sure, just let me know if you need help."

Did I need help booking a flight to Scotland with my husband because his grandfather was dying? Maybe? "Thanks."

She offered me a gentle smile. "You know, I thought Taylor Savage getting married was ridiculous. And a bad idea. But he's different with you. I think you're good for him."

I must've been in shock. So much so that I took myself right to the open bar and poured a nice big glass of wine as the players took the ice and the crowd cheered. All I heard was a roaring in my ears at the thought of what Taylor had been going through all alone.

12

BECCA

WATCHING my husband on the ice was something else. He was a force to be reckoned with, and he did his job as though he was born for it. The man was incredibly focused, fast, and powerful as he flew across the rink. He scored goal after goal, assisting Byrne three times and making an absolute mockery of the other team's defense. By the time the game was over, I was cheering along with the fans, on my feet, laughing and smiling with Scarlett right beside me.

"It seems like being married to a hockey player isn't so bad after all," she teased.

I shrugged. "He's okay."

"Sure, that's the word."

"It's really good to see you," I said, wrapping

my arm around her as we watched the crowd exit the arena now that the game was over.

"You see me almost every day."

"I know, but I used to see you even when we weren't working. Now I only see you up to your elbows in fondant."

"Honestly, I think it was good for me to move out. I should have even before you and Savage got married."

"I don't know why you keep saying that."

"You and Clara treat me like this delicate baby bird. Like I need protecting."

"You do need protecting."

"I'm a grown-up, just as you are. I can take care of myself, and I should. That's my point. So you impulsively marrying a sexy hockey player gave me a reason to start my life. Thank you for that."

I understood where she was coming from. But also, I hated that my sister thought she was some kind of burden. She was far from it. My sisters were everything to me. They were all I had, and it bothered me that they didn't realize it.

"I hope you know you could have lived with me forever. I would have had zero problems with it."

"I know."

Ten minutes later, Taylor poked his head through the door, his hair damp, his skin smelling like the Dove body wash I bought on my monthly Costco runs. Something about that made me smile. He wasn't hurting for money, but he'd rather use the stuff I bought. It was frustrating that this man could make my heart go squishy when I had so vigorously fought to protect myself. All he'd had to do was come into my life and offer to save me, and I was panting for him. I was pathetic.

The worst part was if I let myself really fall for him, I'd lose a lot more than money. He'd have every breakable part of me at his disposal, and that was terrifying.

"Well, wife, did you enjoy your first go-round with the NHL?"

And just like that, I was a puddle of stupid hormonal goo, because his question wasn't asked with the air of overconfidence I expected from him. It was full of nervous energy, like he was worried.

"I had a good time, surprisingly. I loved it."

"Really?" Excitement flickered in his eyes. "You did?"

"Yeah. I did. I'm sad the season's over. I want to come to another game."

"Don't worry, it's not a long break. Practices will start soon."

He left the obvious flaw out of that statement because we wouldn't be together for next season. But I pushed that thought aside and didn't let myself dwell on the fact I'd be losing him.

Scarlett nudged me. "Well, you two lovebirds . . . isn't there some kind of last game of the season party or something we shouldn't be missing?"

"Yes, in fact, there is," Taylor said, holding out his hand. "Be my date?"

"I'm not really dressed for a party."

"Trust me, my darling, you look absolutely perfect."

Scarlett sighed. She actually sighed. "I love it when you call her that."

"Oh, I've got lots of names for her. But my date is my favorite. Come on, hen."

I instinctively bristled against the stupid hormonal urge to melt into a puddle. "I didn't say I'd go. What if I don't want to be with you tonight?"

"You want me. You know you do."

"I don't want you."

"Liar."

I scoffed. "You're ridiculous."

"Admit it, you like me just a wee bit."

Scarlett snickered. "Yeah, come on, lass. Don't you like him a wee bit?"

"Scarlett, you traitor."

She shrugged. "I'm not trying to help you."

"I like her." Taylor chuckled.

"Oh, you're trouble," I grumbled.

Taylor smirked and threw his arm around my shoulder, tucking me into his side.

"You knew I was trouble the first time you saw me."

"That's true. I should have left you at the ferry terminal."

"Now let's go, Tinkerbell. I have a party to go to, and it is a requirement that I have my wife by my side."

"Oh, is it?"

"Yes. There might be photographers."

"Well, we wouldn't want to let the photographers down, now would we?"

"Definitely not."

"Especially if it means they'll be given the chance to take my photo in your number?"

"Aye."

"You're nothing if not predictable."

"And you're nothing if not startlingly beautiful."

"If you're not careful, you're going to make her fall in love with you," Scarlett said.

My stomach clenched at the thought. Would it be so bad to fall in love with Taylor Savage? I had mixed feelings. On the one hand, Taylor was everything I'd ever thought I wanted. On the other, he was the thing that was the most dangerous to me. I didn't know how to reconcile myself with both.

He led me to his car, held open the door, and I slipped in beside him, loving the scent of leather and . . . him that permeated the small space. "You looked really good out there. I see why you love it so much."

"I can't tell you what it means to me to know you were there watching. Cheering for me."

"I have to ask you something." I swallowed past a lump in my throat, knowing we were going to broach a subject he had deliberately kept from me.

"Anything. Go ahead, I'm yours."

"Why didn't you tell me about your grandfather?"

The way his knuckles turned white on the steering wheel said everything I needed to know.

"There's nothing to tell."

"Cut the crap. I know he's dying."

"He's been dying for years." He leaned his head back, heaving a sigh. "I'm sure you've gathered that my dad and I don't get on."

"Yes. I put that together."

"My granddad and I, that's a different story. He's the best man I ever knew."

"So why wouldn't you want to talk about it?"

"Not everyone wants to sit around and rehash all the crap things in their life. Especially when they're going to absolute shit."

"So you think it's better to just not talk about it at all? That's not gonna help with anything."

"It'll help me if I pretend it's not happening."

"Taylor, don't play with me."

He scoffed. "You lassies always want to talk

about things. You really want to sit here and listen to me moan about my life?"

"Yes, Taylor. We can discuss it. You and I can talk about it because I'm here for you."

Taylor took a deep breath and stared into my eyes, swallowing hard before he spoke. "He got sick five years ago, and we thought he'd turned a corner, but Mum sent me an email updating me a week ago. He's only got a few months. She wanted me to come for a visit soon. I haven't decided what to do."

"I think you should. I didn't get to see my parents before they died, and I wish I would have been able to tell them what they meant to me."

"I'm going to go. I need to."

"Alone?"

"I'll be fine."

"I know." Then I took his hand. "You don't have to do everything on your own."

"What, are you gonna cash in on a free trip to Scotland?"

I jerked back like he'd hit me. I knew it was a taunt, but I already felt uncomfortable that he'd given me money for upholding my end of the bargain.

"That's not what I meant." He dragged a hand through his hair. "Sorry. I can be a prick when I'm fighting with my emotions."

"I don't know if I could go even if you wanted me to."

"I do, though. If I'm honest, I really want to have you there. It's going to be hard to see him and know it's the last time."

"When are you planning to go?"

"I'm not sure. I haven't thought that far ahead."

"I'll see what I can do."

"Thank you, hen. I mean it."

Instead of heading toward Ethan's house, Taylor turned to take us back to the ferry.

"Where are you going?"

"I just want tonight to be us. Is that all right?"

"If you're sure." But a big part of me was thrilled he'd rather spend time with me.

"We can have our own celebration at home. We could order in. Make some dessert?"

I grinned. Thinking of the congratulatory cupcakes I baked for him, complete with his number and mini hockey sticks decorating them. "I might have already put something together."

"Are you serious?"

I shrugged. "I like a special occasion. Sue me."

"Now I know you really do care."

"Don't get too cocky. One of the cupcakes has cardamom in it."

That was a lie, but he didn't need to know that.

TAYLOR

"Do you have something you need to tell me, son?" My mum's voice was sharp and knowing.

I'd been on this end of her anger more than my fair share growing up. The real kicker was, she knew the answer to her question. She just didn't want to come out and say it.

No, that opportunity was reserved solely for me. The perpetrator. "What have you heard?"

"Oh, you know exactly what I've heard. Now out with it."

I sighed. "All right. Two months ago, I got married."

"My only son got married without telling me. How do you think that makes me feel? How do you think that makes the entire family feel? Taylor, this is a major change in your life, and you weren't even going to tell us."

She was right. I was trying to keep it under wraps as much as I could. Because I wanted to avoid this scene. "It's not a big deal."

"Not a big deal? Yes, it is. This is the biggest moment of your life. This is a woman who's going to have your children, who's going to give me wee grandbabies. Oh, Taylor. I had to find out about it from Penny Patmore. Down at the butcher's . . . Penny Patmore. Do you ken what she said? She said, 'Oh, look, there's your wee lad all grown up. And married to such a pretty little girl. Even if she is American.'"

She wasn't wrong. Becca was incredibly pretty. "Mum. It was a surprise. It happened out of the blue. I wasn't sure how to tell you."

"It's simple. I'll tell you exactly how you're supposed to do it. You ring up your mum. And then you tell her, Mum, I got married. This is my wife's name. Here's her picture. And then I can say, congratulations. When do I get to meet her?"

And there it was. I didn't want my family to fall in love with Becca, because they would. It was hard not to. I was struggling with it myself. "Becca is very busy. She has a bakery that she runs with her sister."

"Oh, I know all about her. I looked her up. The sister of the team's owner. So scandalous. A whirlwind romance. How appropriate. Just like your father and me."

I bristled. We were nothing like my father and her. I didn't want to be anything like him. "Mum, I'm sorry. With everything going on with granddad, I just didn't think it was the right time to tell you."

"Are you off your head? Happy news is exactly what he needs. I've already told them we'll be celebrating your marriage when you visit next week."

"Mum, she's not coming."

"Don't be ridiculous. Of course she's coming. She's your new bride after all."

"I just don't think she can get the time off work."

"The time off work. Are you not a professional athlete, son? Surely she can afford to take some time off work to come meet her new family. To give your grandfather one last happy memory before he departs from this world. That poor man has been through so much. And he loves you so much."

An arrow straight through my heart couldn't have hurt more. She knew exactly what she was doing.

"I'll talk to her. See if we can make it work."

"Good. Your room is all ready for you. And I hope you do make it work because I've already ordered the flowers."

"The flowers?"

"Yes. For your wedding party."

"Wedding party."

"Of course. Did you think we wouldn't have a ceilidh to celebrate?"

Bloody hell.

She continued. "Be sure to phone me as soon as you know. I'll let my new daughter-in-law in on the secret that her new mum won't take no for an answer."

"Hell's bells," I grumbled after she hung up. I didn't know what I was thinking, trying to hide it. I was the source of big news in the small town where I grew up. It was the sort of place where people still spoke Gaelic. And threw ceilidhs and festivals and had the Highland Games. No one made it big in our town. Until me.

"What put that look on your face?" Becca asked as she came in the kitchen door and made a beeline straight for the pot of coffee on the counter.

She had a soft dusting of either flour or powdered sugar across the bridge of her nose. I couldn't help myself; I reached out and brushed it off.

"I just spoke to my mum."

Immediately she set down her cup, even though she had barely brought it to her lips. The look of worry on her face tightened something inside my chest.

"Oh no. Is it your grandfather?"

"In a manner of speaking. It's all right, he's fine. Well, as fine as he could be, but he's still holding on."

"Okay, so why do you look like your world's about to end?"

"It's not, it's just . . . I may have made a bit of a misstep with this marriage."

Her brows furrowed. "I don't understand."

"Our arrangement is more complicated than I took into account."

"Why?"

"Everyone in my town knows. And my mum thinks it's real."

"She does?"

"Yes. They all do. I don't know why I thought we could fly under the radar over there, but the cat's out of the bag, and well, lass, they want to meet you."

"That might not be a good idea, Taylor. If they meet me . . ."

"There's no way they won't fall in love with you."

Her cheeks turned pink. "I don't want to hurt them when we tell them the truth."

"I can call her and tell her you can't make it. She was planning . . . Well, they planned the whole wedding festival and party. They want you to help bring my grandfather some sense of peace and a happy memory before he dies. I told her you were too busy."

"Oh, great. So now she thinks your wife is a cold, unfeeling American bitch."

I chuckled. She didn't know how right she was. "But it shouldn't matter because they'll never see you again. We'll get divorced. We'll be done with it."

"But I'll know, and try as I might, I can't help but care what other people think of me. It's a weakness, I know, but it doesn't make it any less true."

"So what do you want to do? You don't seriously want to come with me. I thought your offer was more to make me feel better than anything else."

"I think I have to. I'll go with you, meet your family, and then go back to normal life."

"So we'll explain it to them when we get there."

"No. What, are you new here? I don't even have parents anymore, and I know that's not a good idea."

I frowned, but she continued.

"Listen, Taylor, here's what we do. We go to Scotland. You give me the grand tour of the country I've never been to—preferably while you wear a kilt—and I charm the plaid off your family, make them happy, pretend I'm deliriously in love with you, and then we part amicably. Who knows? Maybe I'll get lucky, and you'll get traded at the end of our year together, and you can use my business as the excuse for our divorce."

Maybe she'd get lucky, and I get traded? I didn't want to move. I liked Seattle. But then more possibilities with her plan tumbled around in my brain. I could prove to my dad that I wasn't a fuckup. I could make my grandfather happy. My mother happy. I could also spend time with Becca, and a big part of me wanted that more than anything.

"Okay, but I'm warning you, I know how this goes. I've seen a rom-com or two in my time."

"Oh yeah?"

"Yeah. You're going to fall so hard, you won't want to let me go when our time is up."

"There's the cocky alphahole."

I waggled my eyebrows. "You know you love him."

"I tolerate him because he's pretty."

Then I winked. "Do you have your passport, love?"

"I do."

"Well then, you'd better let Scarlett know you're taking two weeks off starting next week."

"And what are we going to do about the bakery?"

"I'll hire staff to cover for you. I'm sure I can get someone."

She let that roll over in her mind, puzzling it all out in her head for a minute before she locked eyes with me. "Okay, let's go to Scotland."

13

BECCA

This was the longest plane ride I'd ever been on. Even flying first class, I needed to get up and stretch my legs. Taylor slept quietly beside me. He'd given me the window seat so I could see as we flew into Edinburgh. I remembered vividly one day when my mother and I had been heading to the grocery store together—I must have been only six, maybe younger—and I asked her why she looked so sad. All she did was sigh and shake her head. The song "Leaving on a Jet Plane" by Jefferson Airplane came on the radio. She turned it up and sang softly while I bopped my head. Then when she parked the car in the parking lot, she turned and looked back at me.

"Marry the man who gives you the window

seat on the plane, sweetie. One who does it without you asking for it."

I never understood what she meant. Until now. She wasn't saying because someone gave you a window seat, you needed to marry them. I'd thought it was such a weird bit of advice when I was little. But now I realized she was saying marry the man who gives you what you need before you know you need it. It unnerved me that Taylor was doing that. That's not what I expected from him.

As we touched down on Scottish soil, Taylor's body tensed. The energy he gave off changed, and his posture went tighter and tighter with every passing moment. As we picked up our rental car, he tensed. As we drove the winding roads through the beautiful landscape, he tensed. His grip on the steering wheel was white-knuckled, his jaw clenched so hard I could see the veins in his neck popping, and when we reached the gated property, he stopped and turned to look at me.

"You don't know what this means. You doing this. And I'm sorry in advance for the welcome you're going to receive."

"I don't know what you're so afraid of."

He didn't answer me, but as the gate slid open, I reached out and placed my palm on his knee, giving it a light squeeze. Something in his shoulders loosened with that bit of contact, so I didn't move my hand, and when we pulled up to the large old estate, I realized there was a lot more to Taylor Savage and his backstory than anyone had ever let on.

"Um, are you like a laird or something?"

He laughed and shook his head. "No, but my granddad is."

"Oh my God. Are you serious?"

"Yeah."

"Well, that's a surprise. Why didn't the media pick up on that?"

"We paid them a very handsome sum of money to keep it quiet."

"Is your real last name Savage?"

"Legally? Yes."

"And what about at birth?"

"No. I come from a long line of McCulloughs."

"So I'm Becca McCullough, then?"

He stiffened. "No. You're Rebecca Savage. And I'm Taylor Savage. And that's all there is to it. You understand? I'll never claim the title."

"So what happens when it passes to you?"

"It won't. I've got a cousin named Hugh, and he will have that great honor."

"My, my, my, the baker and the rake sounds like a romance novel if I ever heard one." I giggled.

"Just tell me one thing."

"What?"

He smirked, a bit of levity brightening his eyes. "Is it a bodice ripper?"

That made my belly flip and tingles build between my thighs. I thought maybe it was.

"I haven't figured it out yet."

"That's much more promising than a no."

"Don't get your hopes up."

"Oh, my hopes have been up since the day I met you and you tried to kill me."

"I thought you let that go. It was an accident!"

A low rumbling laugh filled the car. "Relax. I'm just taking the piss. I know you'd never really try to kill me." He opened his door and I reached for mine, but he stopped me. "No. Wait right there." Then he walked around and opened the door for me, holding out a hand to help me out. "What kind of a husband would I be if I didn't let my chivalry shine through every now and again?"

"Careful, I could get used to a certain lifestyle, and then where will you be?"

"I could get used to providing you a certain kind of lifestyle. You won't see me complaining."

God, if only I could trust that this would be how things truly would be for us.

"Taylor?"

"Becca?"

"Do you think . . ." I bit my lip and worked up the courage to ask him what I wanted to know.

"What, hen?"

"Do you think you could wear a kilt for me?"

"Do you really want me to?"

"Absolutely."

"Then it would be my pleasure. But I want to warn you, everything they say about kilts is true."

I grinned. "That's what I was hoping for."

TAYLOR

Squeals of joy from the two six-year-old terrors as they raced down the stairs toward me had a smile pulling my lips upward without a second thought. My nephews, Hamish and Harry. It had been ages since I saw them last, but I video chatted with them nearly every weekend.

"Oh, it's the double Hs. What kind of trouble are you two lads up to already?"

"We came to see the woman who made an honest man out of you."

"Hamish, Mummy said not to repeat everything we hear."

"What? I didn't repeat the part about how he probably already got her up the duff. What does that mean anyway? What's the duff?"

Absolute mortification settled in my chest.

"Up the duff means pregnant like Mummy is," my sister said, her hand resting gently on the swell of her lower belly.

"But the real question is," I said. "Is it twins this time?"

My sister sighed. "It better not be, or that

husband of mine is going to find himself having his swimmers cut off."

Marie's hazel eyes trailed past me and landed on the woman standing just behind me. "Is this her?" she asked, no malice in her tone, just curiosity.

Becca threaded our fingers together as I pulled her forward. "Aye, this is her. Becca, meet my wee baby sister. And apparently master procreator, Marie."

"It's nice to meet you," Becca said, holding out a hand for Marie to shake. But my sister let out a snort before pulling her in and wrapping her arms around her.

"None of that. You're a McCullough now. That means incredibly over-affectionate, loud, boisterous, and completely disrespectful of privacy. Welcome to the clan."

Becca shot me a worried glance over her shoulder, and I simply shrugged. All of it was true. I hadn't known a moment's peace growing up, and it was a brave soul who willingly joined the McCullough clan.

"So . . ." Hamish said. "Am I going to have a cousin?"

Becca turned her attention from my sister and knelt down so she was Hamish's height.

"Let's see, you look like a Hamish to me. Is that right?"

He gave her a wide, gap-toothed grin. "That's me. Hamish William McCullough."

"My, that's a big name."

"It's twenty-three letters."

Becca made a show of pretending to count them. "It sure is."

"So, are you having a baby?"

Becca shook her head. "No, no babies."

Hamish wrinkled up his face. "Aw, Mum. You told me I'd get a cousin."

"I said perhaps you would get a cousin. Eventually." I could see the embarrassment on my sister's face. She sent me an apologetic glance and then mouthed, "I'm so sorry," before ushering the children away and leaving Becca and me alone.

"This place is so much different from what I expected." Becca smiled as she took in our surroundings.

"What did you expect?"

"I didn't think it would be something so close to a castle. I was expecting a modest house in the city."

"No, we're country folk. My family has always been. We like the wide open spaces and the rolling hills."

"Are you happy living in such close quarters, then? In cities like you have been?"

"I don't mind it if it means I get to play hockey. I'll live anywhere."

"What if you got traded to somewhere new and hated it?"

"Then I'd do a lot of traveling in the off-season."

"And what about if you fell in love with a place and didn't want to leave?"

She didn't know it, but she was hitting every one of my pain points. I swallowed down the unease. "Then I'd hope never to be traded."

"Is that realistic?"

"Not usually, but some people stay on teams for most of their career."

I took her by the hand and led her up the stairs, following the long hallway until I found the door to the bedroom where I grew up.

"Fair warning, hen. This may still be a shrine to sixteen-year-old Taylor."

"Oh, am I going to find Playboys hidden under your mattress?"

"No, but you might find posters of Wayne Gretzky everywhere."

Her smile was magnetic. And it made me wish I could kiss her. Instead I took that opportunity to reach out and tuck the stray lock of hair behind her ear. "He's like the Michael Jordan of hockey, right?"

A bark of laughter left me, and I nodded. "I guess you could say that."

I opened the door and was surprised and a

little disappointed to find Mum had redecorated. Instead of a small single bed with Star Wars sheets and posters of my favorite hockey teams, the room was modern, with a queen-size bed, a plush rug, even a small chair near the window with a bookcase next to it and a cozy reading lamp.

"I was promised Wayne Gretzky."

"It looks like Mum has been busy. To be fair, I haven't been home in quite a few years. It's not like I expected her to keep it a shrine to me or anything. But part of me mourns the loss of that piece of nostalgia I was hoping to walk back into."

"Well, it's still nice."

"Are you sure you're going to be okay with this? Us sharing a bed. Sharing a room."

"We're grown adults, Taylor. Nothing will happen we don't want. It's not like you can ruin me or anything. We're already married."

"I will endeavor to keep my hands to myself." I held up my hands in a gesture of innocence.

"And I will attempt to keep myself from seducing you with my feminine wiles."

How did I tell her that just being around her seduced me? The answer? I didn't. It wouldn't make anything easier.

As if proving my point, she sat on the bed, bouncing a couple of times, her tits doing amazing things in that T-shirt and making my cock thicken behind my fly. This was going to be an uncomfortable two weeks.

"The bathroom's attached, so if you want to freshen up or anything, feel free. You don't have to worry about sharing with anyone."

"Except for you."

"Except for me, but I won't take up too much time."

"Does this mean I get to listen to your shower karaoke every morning? Because let me tell you, that is a special treat."

"What? I always made sure you were out in the bakery."

"Well, I don't know if you know this, but the window to the bathroom is over the garage."

"So you could hear me?"

"Every single off-key note."

"Did it make you think about me? Naked, soapy, and wet?"

I expected her to laugh and look away. Instead she bit her lower lip and cast her gaze right on my package.

"It might have crossed my mind a time or two."

"Oh, really? That is interesting indeed."

"Stop it. Like you never pictured me naked."

"Oh, I have." I closed my eyes. "I'm doing it right now. I wonder, do the curtains match the drapes?"

Something soft hit me right in the face. A throw pillow.

"Those are meant to be decorative. Just because they're called throw pillows doesn't mean you actually throw them."

"Really? It seems like they work just fine for me."

I close my eyes again. "Oh, I'm sorry. I couldn't hear you. I was too busy picturing you naked."

"Taylor, stop it." She laughed.

I opened my eyes to find her standing in front of me. Gaze banked with something that curiously resembled hunger.

"Maybe if you're lucky, you'll get to see the real thing and figure out if your imagination is as good as your creative skills in the bakery."

"How do you know I haven't already seen you naked?"

I narrowed my eyes, sure she's seen my cock before, but I'd never been starkers in front of her. Had I? "Have you been spying on me in the shower? Is there a camera set up in there? You know that's illegal, right? That's voyeurism."

She grinned. "Oh, how quickly you forget about the charity calendar."

That's right. The hockey hotties calendar I and a few other teammates took part in. I got to be Mr. February, and yes, I posed fully nude except for a heart-shaped box of chocolates I held in front of my junk. "Don't tell me you have a calendar."

"Of course I do. My sister gave them to both of us for Christmas. She thought it was hilarious."

"And who was your favorite month?"

"Well, it was a toss-up."

"What?" I was on my way to being offended.

"I'm kidding. February, of course. Your tattoos really stood out."

"Well, that's just not fair."

"What isn't?"

"You've seen all of me. I want to see all of you."

"Sorry, you're out of luck. Besides, you got naked for charity. Anyone who bought that can see you."

"Most of me. The important bits were covered. Consider this charity to me. I'm buying you—" I cut myself off at the look in her eyes. "Oh, lass, I'm sorry. I was just joking. I took it too far."

She shut down, her brow furrowing. "Don't call me a whore for taking money from you."

"I didn't mean it like that. I'm sorry."

Her shoulders stiffened. "No, that's fine. Maybe that is what I am."

I was across the room in two seconds flat, pulling her against my chest without even thinking about it. "I'm not buying you. I'm not paying you to do anything with me or be anyone you don't want to be."

"You're paying me to be your wife."

"We're helping each other. That's different. I'm investing in your business. I don't expect you to take off your clothes for me. Yes, we need to pretend that we're in love while we're here, but that's as far as it goes. I don't expect anything more."

Surprisingly, she didn't release me. Just held me closer and nestled her face into my chest.

"Okay. I'm sorry I freaked out."

"It's fine. You didn't freak out."

"Yeah, I did. Let's go downstairs. There's still a lot of house for you to show me."

"True. And the grounds, and the stables, and the gardens."

"Oh, stables?"

I cocked a brow. "That piqued your interest? Aye, stables. Do you fancy a ride?"

"If I get the chance to see you on a horse, sign me up."

I released her, then gave her a little swat on the arse. "Go get yourself cleaned up. I'll meet you downstairs. I'm sure Mum has already laid out an entire platter of snacks for us. She's not happy unless she's feeding someone."

"Okay. I won't be long."

"I'll be waiting." I winked at her and couldn't

stop myself from smiling as she headed into the bathroom.

An hour later, when she still wasn't down with the rest of us, I went upstairs to check on her. The sun had dipped below the horizon, casting everything in the warm glow of twilight. As I inched the door open, I found her curled up on her side, sound asleep, still dressed in the clothes she'd worn on the airplane. She was snoring softly, and I couldn't keep from reaching down and grabbing the blanket folded neatly at the edge of the bed. I tugged it up and covered her.

"Goodnight, hen. I'll see you in the morning."

I couldn't help myself. I dropped a kiss to her temple and inhaled her perfume. There wasn't anything I didn't like about this woman, and that was no surprise to me because I'd been attracted to her since the day we first met. But now, watching her in my family's home, interacting with my relatives, I knew I was in too deep.

But I didn't see a damn thing wrong with that.

BECCA

The soft click of the bedroom door shutting woke me from a sound sleep. A blanket was draped over my body, the spicy scent of Taylor washing over me.

"Taylor?" I whispered.

"Shh, lass. It's late. Go back to sleep."

"What time is it?" I fumbled for my phone, which I'd put on the charger next to the bed.

"It's two in the morning." He sat down on the side of the bed and rested his elbows on his thighs.

"And you're just coming to bed?"

"I was catching up with my sister and her husband. Time slipped by."

The scent of Scotch on his breath told me exactly how time had done that. Then it hit me.

"Oh, shit. Dinner. I'm so sorry. I just laid down and planned to close my eyes for a minute."

He chuckled. "We waited for you, but after you didn't come down, Mum told us to go ahead."

"Why didn't you come wake me up?"

"Oh, lass, I tried. Mum threatened to disown me if I disturbed you. She said you needed your beauty sleep and that dinner would keep and not to wake you if I wanted to see morning."

"Wow. The great Taylor Savage, taken out at the knees by his mommy."

"You clearly don't know her." He reached over his head to pull off his shirt in that sexy way men had, and I lost track of what he was saying because . . . God bless hockey.

The way he moved, like it was second nature,

like men were taught this skill in after-school classes during their formative years, had me biting my lower lip and watching him intently. I could just picture it. A coach giving notes. 'Here's how to seduce someone, boys. Make sure you flex too. Really give 'em a show.'

I swallowed a little moan at the sight of him, that shirt slipping off his body, muscles shifting as he moved, moonlight casting shadows in all the right places.

"Thirsty, lass?" His low rumble had my mouth dry but my pussy wet.

"Yes."

He grinned as he unzipped his suitcase and pulled out a pair of pajama pants and a white shirt. "Let me get changed, and we'll go downstairs for a wee nip, yeah?"

"Aren't you tired?"

He shrugged. "You're awake, which means you're going to talk my ear off when you realize you can't get back to sleep. Better to just accept it."

I shivered as I sat up, and the blanket fell to my waist. "It's cold in here."

"Old house. Drafty."

I didn't miss the way his gaze focused on my chest. Especially after I remembered I'd taken my bra off as soon as he'd left me in the room. There was nothing better than taking off that torture device after a long day.

"Let me . . . get you something to wear."

My thin T-shirt did nothing to hide the stiff peaks of my nipples, and if his tense shoulders were any indication, he wanted a closer look at them.

"Do my nipples make you uncomfortable, Taylor?"

"When you're waving them about like that, aye, they do. Especially when I don't get to play with them."

I could let him. That thought ran through my mind before anything else. But then I remembered why that would be a bad idea. Taylor and I were two opposing forces going in completely different directions. There was no course that led us down the same path. He wasn't going to stay in Seattle forever. He'd find something better, someone who could travel with him, who could be everything he really needed. I was just a temporary solution to a problem. He wanted off the dating app, and I needed a new kitchen. Simple.

Instead of continuing to check me out, he surprised me by handing me a hoodie. "Here, put this on. You're not going to get any warmer sitting there in that shirt."

"You're afraid of my boobs, aren't you?"

"No, lass. I like your boobs. A whole fucking lot. But I also don't think I'll be able to give you the attention you deserve if I can see them through your shirt. I've had far too much Scotch for that level of restraint."

I couldn't contain my giggle. "Are you afraid you'll compromise my reputation?"

"Well, seeing as we're man and wife, there's nothing to compromise. I could drive the headboard into the wall all night, and no one would say a damn word. But I'm not willing to cross those boundaries we set because you're . . ."

"I'm, what?"

"As much crap as we give each other, Becca, you're important to me. I want to make you happy for the time we're together."

I slipped his hoodie over my head, loving the way his scent enveloped me. "I'm happy."

"Alone in a marriage we arranged?"

"I'm not alone, but I also don't mind being single. I'm not afraid to exist on my own."

He locked gazes with me. "Neither am I, but I also don't want to go through my whole life without someone to share it with."

"You've definitely had some Scotch if you're talking like this."

His soft huff of laughter had me sliding my hand on top of his. "That's why my Mum always calls it her truth serum. But alcohol or no, I'm being straight with you. There's nothing wrong with falling in love, Becca. When you find the right one, it'll happen and you'll see. I know it's not me, and I'll always regret that fact, but one day, you'll find him. The right man for you. And you'll tell him about this mad Scottish hockey player you spent a year with."

There was such an undercurrent of melancholy in his voice as he made his speech. Almost like he wasn't even talking to me, but convincing himself of the truth before the story was over. Preparing himself for the inevitable.

"Why don't we just lie down, Taylor? I don't need a drink. I'm still pretty tired."

He nodded but didn't say anything else. Then stood and reached for a pillow, but I placed a hand on his forearm, stopping him.

"You don't need to sleep on the floor. There's plenty of room."

He cocked a brow. "Are ye serious?"

"I trust you to keep your hands to yourself. And you've had enough to drink. You need a comfortable bed and plenty of sleep."

"I take back everything bad I ever said about you."

"You were talking shit, Shrek?"

He snorted. "Oh, real original. Call the Scot Shrek. It would only be worse if you threw out the Braveheart instead."

"I could've called you Jamie. Y'know, like from Outlander."

Tossing his big body on the bed, he sighed. "Aye, you could, Sassenach. And I could show you exactly why there are so many romance novels written about us highlanders."

A little shiver ran down my spine at the promise in his words and I decided not to comment on the fact that he'd always said Edinburgh was his home. But now that I knew his family history, maybe it was just easier for him to hail from Edinburgh in the eyes of everyone else.

"Maybe later."

His palm skated across my lower back. "Come lie with me. Try to sleep, or you'll never get adjusted to the time difference."

I sighed. "I need to change into my pajamas first. I can't sleep in jeans."

"Go ahead. I won't peek." He slapped his hand over his eyes.

"There's a perfectly good bathroom for me to change in. No need for you to use up every ounce of your chivalry in one night."

The only response I got was a low, rumbling groan.

"Don't complain."

"M'not. You were keeping me warm. Hurry up with your changing, wife. It's cold in this old castle."

Honestly, he was right. I was chilled deep into my bones as I rifled through my suitcase and pulled out a pair of pajamas. In a few short minutes, I was changed, my teeth brushed and face washed. But by the time I crawled under the covers, Taylor was sound asleep, softly snoring. He'd probably be hungover tomorrow, but I was glad he'd had the chance to catch up with his sister. She obviously meant the world to him. Seeing him in this light was already changing how I thought about him.

As I snuggled down in the bed, he made a happy sound, like a contented sigh, and rolled toward me, one hand sliding onto my waist. I didn't stop him. I wanted his touch. His warmth. This version of him who was open and kind.

"Goodnight, Tink," he murmured.

"Goodnight, Hook."

14

TAYLOR

I DIDN'T WANT to take advantage of her being tired or half asleep, but the way she moved against me and grabbed my hand, pulling it to her lower belly, was torture. Then she moaned my name and pushed my palm down, down, down between her thighs.

"More, Taylor. Touch me."

When I slipped my fingers between her legs, her little groan had me nearly coming apart.

But I stilled. I made myself back away, taking slow, deep breaths as I worked to calm myself. The last thing I needed was for her to think I wasn't genuine in my affection. I had to rein in my desire.

All I wanted was her. If I was honest, I'd needed her for so long, but she made up her mind about me because of my own mistakes. I hadn't kissed her since our wedding, even though I wanted to. I'd come close a few times but hadn't given in.

I needed to go. If I didn't, I'd do something stupid, like kiss her.

She wriggled closer, whispering, "Taylor."

"You'd better tell me to stop, because I am desperate to feel you, hen." I pressed my lips to her ear and whispered, "I'm dying for you, Becca, and I'm at your mercy."

She sighed my name again and tilted her hips so her perfect arse rocked into my throbbing erection. "Don't stop, Taylor. Please don't stop."

"Oh, lass, there's only one thing I'd ever want to hear from your lips other than that."

"What is it?"

I couldn't tell her I wanted to hear her say she loved me. That would scare her away, and I'd just gotten her to stop hating me.

"Are you sure you want this?"

"I need . . . I need you to make me feel good. It's been so long."

"When was the last time a man made you feel good, sweetheart?"

She stayed silent for a minute before rolling her hips again, then she took my hand and slid it inside her pants, under the waistband of her panties, to the neatly trimmed thatch of hair that hid her pussy from me.

"Since I slept with a man? Or since someone made me..."

"How long since you slept with someone?"

"A year."

I stared at her, completely shocked. "You mean to tell me you haven't been with anyone since before our first date?"

"No, I haven't."

Masculine pride washed through me, followed quickly by regret. I hadn't even had a chance to get her off more than once before I'd fucked things up with her. But then again, neither had any other bloke.

"Becca," I whispered, gently sliding my finger over her clit and making her sigh.

"Yes?"

"Will you let me make you feel good?"

She moaned, "God, yes. Fuck me."

The sound of her pleasure had me twitching in my pants. I wanted to drag that sound from her, save it, and make it my fucking ringtone. I circled her clit gently, slowly tapping it, then began a careful slide between her lips until I found her hot, slick entrance.

"Can I? Can I go inside?"

She parted her thighs for me and nodded. When I sank one finger into her, she gripped my arm tight enough that I worried I'd hurt her.

"Are you okay?"

"Yes," she whispered. "You just . . . you're different than I thought you'd be."

"Am I? How did you think I'd be?"

"Selfish. Focused on yourself. Rough. Aggressive. Everything an alpha male is supposed to be."

"Well, lass, a true alpha protects what's his, cares for her, makes sure she's happy above all else. Tell me." I pulled my finger out and began rhythmically rubbing her clit. "Are you happy? Are you satisfied?"

She began rocking her hips in time with my attention.

"How does that feel, Becca? Are you going to come?"

"Not yet." Her arse rubbed against me and had my balls tight and aching. I needed her to come. I wasn't going to last.

"Feels so good," she whimpered. "You make me feel good."

"Yes. Come on, baby. Use me and make yourself come."

She began rocking those hips back and forth in earnest, and I just let her fuck herself on me. My lips found the shell of her ear and trailed down to the lobe, where I bit down gently, and that was all she needed.

She came with a hoarse cry, shattering violently, and everything in me was laced with pride for what I had just done for my wife. I gave her pleasure, and there was nothing more satisfying than that.

BECCA

Taylor wasn't in bed when I woke up the next morning, even though it was bright and early. I hadn't expected that after he'd been up so late the night before. Not to mention after he'd taken care of me the way he did, how he got me back to sleep...

I shivered thinking of it.

The house was quiet, sleepy, and even though it was large, I was easily able to remember my way to the kitchen. After having a cup of tea to wake myself up, I headed outside into the pale gray morning. The country air was clean, and the only sound was the chirp of birds and the rustle of the breeze through trees. The McCullough property was extensive, full of hills and trails. Great for exactly what I was doing. A long, contemplative walk.

I had a lot to think about. I had a lot to consider after the line we crossed last night, but part of me—a very dominant part—screamed that all I was doing was overthinking this. That it didn't matter in the grand scheme of things whether the two of us had sex. But then there was my heart, which had been broken once before. So badly I didn't think I'd recover. That part begged for protection. Warned that the things Taylor made me feel were just as strong, if not stronger, than the ones that had broken me.

I followed the path as I explored. It took me away from the house and around the back, where I found a concrete pad. Letting my thoughts carry me away, I pictured a young Taylor skating, practicing, the spark of his future coming to life right there. It made me smile to think of his nephews and how wild they were. Was he like that? A freckle-faced, precocious wee lad?

I hadn't seen Taylor's father yet. Apparently he'd been called away to tend to some business. I wondered if his being gone was a good thing or if it was just delaying the inevitable.

Two rowdy dogs bounced toward me out of the tall grass, startling me. Oh God. What if they bit me? I was new. I was trespassing in their minds.

But instead of growling and barking, they came up to me, wagging their tails, tongues lolling to the side. I giggled as I knelt and petted them both. The biggest one stuck his nose in my face and began licking my cheek. Better than ferociously knocking me back on my ass, I guessed.

"Charlie, stop it now. Get off the poor wee lass."

A tall, frail-looking man stood at the edge of the grass, a walking stick in one hand.

"Oh, they're fine. A welcome sight, actually. I was getting kind of lonely."

"Are you looking for Taylor, then?"

"Am I that obvious?"

"Yes, he's your husband. You're in a strange new place. He left you alone. If I were you, I'd be looking for him too."

"Do you know where he is?"

"Aye."

"You must be his grandfather."

"That I am."

"Am I supposed to bow or something? Aren't you like royalty?"

"No. And if you call me my laird, I'll sic one of these dogs on you."

"Okay, what do I call you?"

"Everyone calls me Mac."

"It's nice to meet you, Mac."

He smiled, but there was pain in his eyes. "It's nice to meet you. I'm only sorry I wasn't here to greet you when you two arrived yesterday."

"Taylor said you were seeing your doctor."

"I was."

"How are you feeling?"

"Dinnae fash yerself, lass. I'm just fine." He shook his head. "My grandson must be madly in love to bring you here. We haven't seen him in so long. I thought he'd never return. Don't blame me. My son can be a right arsehole."

"Taylor might have mentioned that."

"He's a good boy. No matter what he tries to make it look like in the papers. He'll be good to you for as long as you'll have him."

My heart gave a little flip at that. "So do you know where he is?"

"Oh, I expect he'll be at the rink."

"The rink?"

"Aye, as soon as I realized how much he loves skating, I had one built on the property."

"And you still have it? You still keep it up?"

"Of course. Besides, his nephews have really taken in their uncle's footsteps. You should see the two of them blazing around like bats from hell."

"Where's the rink?"

He pointed down the path in the direction I'd been going. "Just keep going that way. You'll run straight into it. I'm sure you'll find him there."

"Do you want me to walk back to the house with you?" I asked, uneasy about leaving a man as sick as him on his own.

"No. I'll be fine. I just have to get back inside before that daughter-in-law of mine catches me. She thinks I can't do anything for myself these days."

I gave him a sweet grin because I didn't know what else to do and then watched him slowly make his way toward the house with the dogs at his heels. A few more minutes of strolling along the path led me to a more modern-looking building. Light glowed through the frosted windows, which told me someone was in there. This had to be the rink.

I opened the door and was hit with a blast of cold air. It reminded me of the first time Taylor took me skating with him. Our ill-fated first date somehow made me smile when I thought of it now. The sound of blades scraping over ice, harsh breaths, and the occasional grunt sent a thrill through me. I'd definitely hit the jackpot.

Instead of announcing myself, I sat on one of the benches and just watched him. Around and around he went, brow furrowed, focus trained on what he was doing, on pushing himself harder and harder. He'd switched to figure eights, cut corners sharp enough they made my head spin. Then he pulled out his hockey stick and a puck before beginning drills with them. I was in awe as he skated as fast as he could while trying to maintain control of the puck, taking shot after shot into the goal set up at one end. But my favorite thing he did was when he used the end of his stick and bounced the puck over and over and over as he skated. He never took his eyes away from the puck once it was out there.

I don't think he would have noticed me if it hadn't been for the delicate little sneeze that escaped me. His gaze laser focused on me; he was breathing hard, drenched in sweat as he skated from one end of the ice to right in front of where I was sitting. He leaned against the boards and gave me a cocky grin.

"Couldn't get enough of me, I see. One orgasm, and now I have you hooked. Is that it?"

My cheeks burned. "I was out for a walk. I ran into your grandfather, who is a lovely man, and he told me where I'd find you. Aren't you tired?"

He shrugged. "Couldn't sleep. I had a lot on my mind."

"You should have woken me up. I could have helped you get back to sleep by relieving some tension."

Something dark and hungry flashed in his gaze as I watched him. "Really?"

"Yes."

What was I doing? This was the opposite of establishing boundaries. This was barreling through them at breakneck speed.

"This is a new development I wasn't expecting. Did you put whiskey in your tea this morning? Is that what's caused this change of heart? Wait, have you put on that cardamom lip stuff of yours?"

"Taylor, I just want to repay you for what you did..."

His expression shut down. "If you think making you come is a chore, you couldn't be more wrong. I'm not keeping score. There's nothing to repay. Don't do anything you feel obligated to do."

Then he shoved off the boards and glided away. I felt like an asshole.

"That's not what I meant," I called, but he waved his hand.

I'd been dismissed. And I fucking deserved it.

15

BECCA

"I'm so happy he found you, Becca," Taylor's mother said as she placed a mug of tea in front of me. It had been a few days since our arrival, and I was finally used to the time change, if still a little bleary-eyed.

By the time I came downstairs, she'd gotten up and was ready and waiting for me in the breakfast nook. I watched the mist of the morning swirl and dance between blades of grass as two dogs played together. A strange mixture of sadness and contentment washed over me.

"We found each other at just the right time. Although the first time we went out, I thought there was no way I'd see him again."

She gave me the sweetest smile. "Oh, I've

heard all about you. He told me the day he met you."

What? He'd told her about me? Excitement and unease curled in my belly. "Really?"

"Oh, aye. He called me that very night. It was afternoon for him. He said Mum, I met a brilliant woman. She hates me. So obviously I'm going to marry her." She brought her mug to her lips with a twinkle in her eye.

"You're teasing me."

"He did," she said, putting her cup down and raising her right hand. "Hand to God, he did. I thought I was dreaming. I had to ask Marie to pinch me."

"How do you know it was me?"

"I don't see anyone else here, do you? Does he have some secret wife stashed away?"

I blushed. "Things with Taylor . . ." I began. God, this was getting much more complicated than either of us planned. "He's complicated. But determined to get what he wants."

"He's always been that. Did he ever tell you the story of the first time he got on the ice?"

I shook my head.

"I was so nervous to see him on those skates, but he worked at it like a champ, and by the time the day was over, even though he'd fallen at least ten times, he was zooming around the rink with no help. We knew then he'd been destined to play."

"But what about carrying on the family name? Wasn't that something your father-in-law and husband were upset about?"

"There's an old adage I hold strong to." I watched her, waiting for what she might say. "The man is the head of the household, but the woman..."

"She's the neck," I finished for her.

She beamed. "Exactly, love. Now what does my son have planned for his beautiful bride today?"

"Divulging family secrets, are we?" Taylor's deep voice coated me in a blanket of arousal and, somehow, comfort.

"Oh yes. A regular, naked running around in nothing but a T-shirt photo display. Adorable."

"Mother."

She burst into laughter, and I followed her.

Taylor stared at us, realization dawning. "Oh, you two are dangerous together."

"Don't worry, Becca, after we get through the wedding party will have a good sit down with the family and show you every single embarrassing photo I took of your husband. He really did enjoy running around bare arsed in the garden when he was a wee one."

Taylor shook his head, huffing in exasperation. "Do you have coffee?"

"Of course I do. Instant coffee is there in the corner. You're really the only one who likes it, but I am almost certain your sister made sure we had freshly ground beans before you arrived."

"Bless you both," he murmured as he made a beeline for the cupboard.

As he busied himself with the coffee, his mum stared at him and cocked a brow, a mischievous smirk on her lips.

"Taylor, why don't you take your bride for a drive so she can see some of the sights? You can show her some of our favorite shops, maybe take her to get something to eat."

He poured his coffee out of the French press and into a mug before raising an empty one in my direction and offering silently to make me one. I nodded. Then he filled mine immediately, doctoring it exactly how I liked it without even asking.

"You two already act like you've been married for years," his mom observed.

"What do you mean, Mum? It's just coffee."

"Oh, my boy. It's so much more than just coffee, but that's beside the point. You two drink up. I'll put together some breakfast while you get ready to go out."

He nodded and smiled, then held out a hand for me. "Come on, hen. If we don't do what she asks, we'll be in trouble. And you don't want to be in trouble with my mum."

I stood, taking his hand and fighting the shiver that ran down my spine at the contact.

Those talented fingers of his had me wishing for more.

We took our coffee upstairs, and he closed the door behind us before taking a seat near the window and snagging a book that was on the small table.

"What are you doing?"

"Well, I'm reading and having my coffee while you get ready. In case you didn't notice, I've already showered and I'm dressed for the day. So I'll just wait here for you."

"You don't want to do something else?"

"Listen, if I go downstairs, I'll have to stare my mum in the face and lie to her again. And as much as I didn't want to admit it, you're right. It's a bad feeling. The lying. I don't want to do it if I can help it."

"We've really gotten ourselves into a situation, haven't we?"

"Aye. And the way I see it, there's only one way to get out of it."

"Do you want to stop?"

"Do you?"

I knew how I should answer, what the smart choice would be. To take the opening and say yes.

"I don't know, Taylor. It's only been a little over two months. Are you tired of me already?"

He sighed and dragged a hand through his

hair before gazing out the window. "Tired isn't the word I'd use."

"Then what?"

"Frustrated."

It broke my heart to know how he was feeling, and it confused the hell out of me. "Oh, okay. I see."

Except I didn't see at all. He got me off our first night here. Whispered sweet words in my ears. Layered kisses everywhere but my mouth. But he wouldn't let me touch him. Was I some sort of obligation? Was that what this was about? I didn't want to look at him for another minute because I was afraid I'd slip up and say something like, I think I'm falling for you. Or worse, we should stay married.

Happily ever after wasn't what the two of us had agreed to. An amicable divorce, a new kitchen for my bakery, a new reputation for him, and a solid way off *Meet-Cupid*.

I went into the bathroom and shut the door before stripping out of my cozy pajamas. I turned on the water and took a moment to let it heat as I stared at myself in the mirror. Maybe I was just swept away by the act he was putting on. Maybe none of this was real, and Taylor was pretending for everyone.

But the way he touched me felt real. The way he'd said my name as I came for him had too.

I pulled back the shower curtain and stepped

into the ancient clawfoot tub, and instead of hot water, shards of ice assaulted my skin. I screamed bloody murder and all but jumped out of the tub. The door swung open, and Taylor stood there, eyes wild, ready to defend me.

"What's happened, lass? Are you all right?" His words caught in his throat as he took in my naked body.

As quick as I could, I snagged a towel and covered myself. "The water . . . so cold."

"Cold water warranted a scream like that?"

"You try jumping in there."

He smirked. "I have to take ice baths as part of my physical therapy. I'm not afraid of a little . . . Jesus, that is cold." He turned the dial a few times, waiting to see if the hot water would come back on, and when it didn't, he frowned. "I better go check the water heater. You should put your clothes on."

"I need to shower," I protested.

"I like you dirty."

My belly flipped over a few times at the implication. He left, and I did my best with a washcloth and soap to at least clean the important parts, even though I was shivering and miserable the whole time. When he returned, I was dressed and applying one final coat of mascara. I looked at him and my breath caught at the attraction I saw in his eyes.

"You look so pretty with your hair up and that little sweater."

I smiled. "Thanks. This color sets off my eyes."

"I think it sets off everything."

"So what's the word about the water heater?"

"Busted. We'll go into town and order a new one from the hardware store, and you should pack your bag."

"What? Why?"

"Because we're going to move ourselves to an inn so you don't have to live with no hot water. At least for the next couple of nights."

"Won't your mom be sad?"

"Nae, it was her idea. I think she wants to give us some alone time."

I swallowed hard. The alone time we'd gotten was few and far between. Taylor's nephews hang on to him like spider monkeys, and he was so good with them. He built Legos with them and chased them around on the grounds. Yesterday afternoon I'd found him at the rink running drills with them, their little hockey sticks absolutely adorable.

"The boys are going to be heartbroken."

"They'll get over it. Besides, I think Mum wants to make sure we actually go experience Scotland since it's your first time here. Something tells me she's afraid we'll spend all our time with the family, and you won't get a chance to fall in love with anything else."

Like you? I wanted to say. But I held my tongue.

An hour later, after saying goodbye to the family, kissing his grandfather on the cheek, and driving into the small town just down the hill, Taylor and I had settled into a romantic and *conveniently* available room above the local pub. They seemed to know we were coming because the room was decorated with rose petals and candles, and there was even a bottle of champagne on ice.

"Do you think your mother broke the water heater on purpose?"

He laughed. "I wouldn't put it past her. She's crafty like that. I also have it on good authority that my father will be arriving home today. So it's very likely she was trying to salvage whatever she could of this experience for you."

"I'm not afraid of him."

"No, and you shouldn't be. But he has a way of sucking the life out of everything. Cutting down everything and everyone around him. Making sure we're all walking on eggshells all the time."

"Why does she stay with him?"

He shrugged. "She loves him, and it must not be all bad, or she wouldn't have stayed."

"My parents hated each other."

"You mentioned they stayed together because of the kids."

"And they kept having kids, so they kept staying together longer. It was a mess."

"Are you afraid of that happening? Is that why you don't believe in love?"

"I never said I don't believe in love."

"Well, it's not hard to put it together."

"I just don't want to get hurt. I don't want to get into a relationship complicated by so many irrational feelings."

"Love is irrational."

"True. And then you add in children..."

"What about children?"

"They complicate everything. You have children. You're supposed to stay together. Give them a stable home."

His expression softened as he poured us each a glass of champagne. "Perhaps that's how it used to be. But don't you think giving them two loving parents who are both happy is more important? Giving them an example of doing what's best is better than giving them an example of making yourself miserable and sacrificing your own happiness."

"Do you want kids?"

"Eventually. I'd like to have them, yes. What about you?"

"I honestly haven't thought about it. It just seems so far off in the future, you know? Like some distant thing I don't have to really think about."

"Like your sister?"

"What do you mean?"

"Well, she just decided one day she wanted a baby."

"Maybe I'll do it when I'm ready. *If* I'm ready, with or without a partner. I'm nothing if not independent."

He chuckled. "You're telling me."

"Hey, you never said you wanted a subservient wife."

"Oh, I don't. I just want you."

The tension in the room grew thick as his gaze fell to my lips, and I caught the flexing of his hand out of the corner of my eye.

"Do you want me, Taylor? Really?"

"You know I do."

"I don't think I do. All I know is that we're skirting this line, and it's making it hard for me to tell what's fantasy and what's reality. Where is the lie? And where's the truth?"

"There's never been a lie on my part, or if there has been, the only lie you believe is that I want this to end."

"What are you talking about?" My heart fluttered, this erratic frantic thing in my chest.

"I want it all. I want you. I want us. I don't want it to be pretend. I fell for you the moment I saw you on the ferry. And I think you fell for me too. But I scared you."

Every word that fell from his lips was true. I never stopped thinking about Taylor Savage even when I pretended I hated him.

"So you want to really . . ."

"Aye, I want to do this with you. We can go as fast or as slow as you want, but I need to know you're mine. Not just in name. I need you to give me every part of you because I'm laying my broken pieces at your feet, hoping you'll help me put them back together."

I was terrified, but at the same time, I had already married him. I'd fallen into his web the moment I agreed to this arrangement. What would the harm be in letting him wrap me up and keep me?

"Promise me something."

"Of course. All you have to do is ask."

"Don't break my heart, Taylor."

"I'd sooner break every bone in my body, wife." He stepped closer, reaching out and cupping my face. "From this moment forward, I belong to you and you me. Are we clear?"

I nodded, never breaking contact with his gaze. "There's no one else for me. It's you."

With his free hand, he took my left and brought the knuckles up to his lips, then kissed my wedding ring. "My wife."

I pressed my palm over his heart. "My . . ." I

hesitated before I could get the word out. "Husband." Then he shifted his hand from my cheek to cup the back of my head as he pulled me against his body and lowered his face until his lips were an inch away from mine. I could hear his ragged breaths. Feel the hammering of his heartbeat under my palm. Sense the need crying for release.

"Becca," he whispered.

A loud banging on the door startled us both. "Bloody hell. What the fuck do you want?" he barked, making me giggle, even as frustration worked its way through my veins.

"I'm sorry, Mr. McCullough."

"Savage," he corrected.

"Right, I'm sorry, Mr. Savage. But your father's here to see you."

Taylor closed his eyes, took a deep breath, and let it out. "I'll be right down. Pour me a pint, will ya?"

"Right away."

"There's a good lad." Then he turned his attention to me. "Rain check?"

I nodded because my throat was too dry to get any words out. "Am I attending this little reunion?"

He nodded. "If you don't mind. I could use someone in my corner."

"I'm always in your corner. I promise."

16

BECCA

Taylor held my hand so tightly, like he was afraid he might lose something special if he let go. It made my heart ache. It was more than obvious that his father made him uncomfortable. He hadn't exactly kept it a secret, but still, witnessing it firsthand was disconcerting. My big, strong Scot was brought to his knees by the one person who was supposed to love him unconditionally.

We descended the stairs into the warm air of the pub. The rich scents of food filling the air made me wish we were simply heading down to enjoy dinner. Instead we were greeted by a tall man with wiry salt and pepper hair and a well-kept beard. He looked just like Taylor, only an older version, like a snapshot of the future. We stopped in front of him. No loving greetings were exchanged. My husband simply reached out and gestured toward his father.

"This is my dad, Andrew McCullough. Dad, I would like you to meet my wife, Becca."

Andrew narrowed his gaze at me, not impressed, clearly, but I really didn't care.

"Well, she's certainly not who I would have chosen for you. But I suppose she is passable."

Taylor stiffened, his grip on my hand tightening.

"It's a good thing you didn't get to choose for him, then, isn't it?" Unable to keep myself from letting my sass free, I offered him a wide grin.

Andrew laughed, but the smile didn't reach his eyes.

"What are you doing here? Why aren't you at the house?"

Andrew sighed. "Your mother and I are taking some time apart."

"Oh, do you mean she caught you cheating . . . again? And she threw you out . . . again?"

"That's none of your business. What I do in my personal life is none of your concern."

"It affects my mother. So it certainly is. It breaks her heart because she loves your stupid arse for God knows what reason."

"You don't understand the seriousness of marriage, or you wouldn't have run off and married the first willing woman you found."

It hurt because it was true, but there was no way I was going to let this puffed-up pompous dick make Taylor doubt himself.

"You know, it was one of the best decisions I've ever made. Somehow he turned out to be a kind, giving, loving person. Clearly the only one I have to thank for that is his mother."

The look in Taylor's eyes had my heart breaking for him.

"The least you could have done was bag a supermodel. But since you're not even on a team that can win a championship, I suppose you just settled for a baker in debt to her eyeballs with no family."

My stomach dropped. So he'd been checking in on me. Of course he had.

"You obviously don't understand this, but not everything is about status and power." Taylor slipped his arm around my waist and held me close.

"One day you'll see it was always about status and power. She'll drop you the minute she gets what she wants."

"And what's that?" I asked.

"A meal ticket. You better check your condoms, son. She's probably poked holes in every single one so she can saddle you with child support for the rest of your life."

"Did you come here just to insult my wife?"

"No, I came here to tell you you can still get out of it. Before it's too late."

"I don't want out of it. I'm all in. Becca is my forever." He pulled me tighter into his side, then leaned his head down to press a kiss to my temple. "Don't bother coming home. I'll tell Mum you got called in for some important meeting. I'm sure she'll believe it. In fact, maybe you should just never come back."

"That's not your decision."

"You're right. It's not. It's hers. And I hope that one day she makes it. Now if you'll excuse us, Becca and I have a long day tomorrow. I think we're gonna call it a night, and Dad? Consider yourself uninvited to the wedding party. We don't need you there."

His grip on me was tight as he turned me back toward the stairs. But not before shouting to the bartender, "Send up a bottle of your best Scotch. Mr. McCullough is paying."

The moment we got through the door to the room, he began pacing and dragging his hands through his hair, muttering under his breath. "Always knew he was a bastard, and the way he talked about you . . ."

"Taylor, don't let him get to you."

"Right. He's a bastard. But we've moved on. He's out of our lives now. I can't believe he said those things, that you had to hear them."

"I've heard worse, believe me. I once was a

teenage girl, remember? The things we say to each other are horrible."

"You don't deserve a single cruel word. Thank you for standing up for me and coming to my rescue."

"I hate that he treats you that way."

"He's right about me . . . about how we started this and—"

I put my fingertips over his lips. "He's not right. Even if this might have started one way, it's turned into something completely different. You and I both know it. It doesn't matter what he thinks."

"Becca," he whispered against my fingers, taking my hand and pulling me into him. "Can we go back?"

"Back where?"

"To where we were before he interrupted our moment."

"You mean where you were about to kiss me?"

"Aye."

"I'd like that a lot. I've been dying for you to kiss me again."

"Fuck."

He threaded his fingers in my hair and brought his lips to mine. Soft and sweet at first, but then I reached up and curled my hands around the back of his neck and moaned against him.

"More, please. I need you."

He deepened the kiss, parting my lips with his tongue, dancing with me. His slight groan had me aching for more. My fantasies about this man were long and detailed, but the reality was so much better. He broke apart from me, breaths coming in heavy pants as he backed away and braced his arms on the small side table.

"Becca, I don't know how much longer I can go without being inside you. I don't want to rush you."

"God, I want that too. I don't want to wait any longer. I feel like the way we've been toying with each other all this time has just been one long foreplay session. I need it to be you, and I need it now."

"Yes," he grunted.

I held up a finger. "First I have something I need to take care of.

He frowned. "What's that?"

"Just be patient, and you'll see." I grabbed my bag and bustled into the bathroom, frantically searching for the sexy lingerie I'd packed just in case.

When I came out, the Scotch must have been delivered because Taylor was sipping from a glass filled with amber liquid and a second one sat in front of him.

"Jesus, what are you wearing?"

My cheeks burned as I toyed with lace trimming the edge of my silk nightie. "I just thought I might have an occasion to wear it."

"You did, did you? Did you think you might find yourself some hot Scot?"

"It looks like I did, doesn't it?"

"Aye." The confident fucker brought his Scotch to his lips and took a long pull. "Then bring your pretty little arse over here and let me inspect you more fully."

Two steps. That was all it took for me to get to him. He sat down his glass with a little growl and tugged his shirt over his head, baring that beautiful muscular chest.

"I can't be sweet, not this first time."

"I don't want you any way other than who you are. Give me the Scottish bad boy you promised me."

I kissed him then. Backing away, I slid down to my knees.

"Becca, you don't have to."

"I want to."

I undid his belt buckle and then unzipped his pants.

"I won't last if you do this."

"We have all night. Besides, I thought Taylor Savage was known for his stamina on the ice and off."

"I suppose we'll put it to the test."

Pulling down his boxer briefs, I grinned as his cock sprang free, long and thick with a vein running along the underside. I wanted to trace it with my tongue. Sliding my fingers across him gently, I groaned when he hissed and his dick jerked. My tongue darted out, catching the drop of his cum that glistened at the tip. When I looked up at him while toying with his sensitive head and making him groan, he shoved his hands in my hair, holding me still.

"God, Becca, your mouth."

And then I sucked him slow and steady, over and over. I took him a little deeper each time until he was at the back of my throat and I couldn't go any farther. But there were still inches to go. So I wrapped my palm around the base of his shaft and stroked in time with the rest of my movements. His thighs trembled as a guttural moan ripped from him.

"Lass, if you don't stop, I'm gonna shoot right in that pretty mouth of yours."

I kept going, fingers brushing his balls, which were already high and tight. Then he was pulsing down my throat, his ragged cries filling the air. But I didn't stop. I sucked and swallowed him down until he finally pulled me off him and dropped to his knees.

"You devious little thing. Lie back and spread your legs. It's my turn."

TAYLOR

"Your turn? For what?"

"To play. You tasted me, now I'm going to taste you. I've been dying to do this since I took you out for the first time."

I lifted her onto the bed, then pulled up until it was just her hips on the edge, her legs hanging down, and then I knelt at her feet.

"Go ahead and scream my name when you need to, hen. No one will hear you, and if they do, it'll just be proof I know how to take care of my wife."

I could have sunk my cock into her then and there. I was already hard again just looking at her, but she deserved more. As much as I'd love to fill her and sate my lust, I touched her tender places, took my fingers and trailed them up her legs, along her inner thighs. As I shoved the silk higher to her waist, she moaned and squirmed under my attention.

"Taylor," she whined. "You're teasing me."

I smiled. "Aye, I am. But only because I like to make you feel good. The same way you do for me."

"But you're teasing me so much. You won't even touch me where I want you the most."

"I'm doing it the right way because we're not there yet."

"And where are we?"

"Right now, we're at the point where you are at my mercy. I am going to savor you."

"What if I don't want to let you savor me? What if I just want to take you inside me?"

"You are going to be the death of me, but I think it might be worthwhile."

I slid my lips along her inner thighs, kissing the soft skin, taking it between my teeth. I loved the way she widened her legs so I could fit my shoulders between them. Hands splayed across her thighs, I spread her open. I kissed her pretty cunt, then paused for long moments before worshiping and teasing her. When I sucked her clit into my mouth as I teased her opening with my fingers, she bucked and writhed, and it wasn't long before she was coming on a ragged cry. Her fingers dug into my hair as she ground my face exactly where she wanted, riding out the last of her orgasm.

"You're perfect," I whispered as I placed myself at her entrance. I couldn't help myself watching as she lay there, her eyes closed, brows pinched. "Open your eyes, Becca. I want to watch you when I sink inside your body for the first time. I want to see it the moment you feel me and know I'm finally taking you."

Her eyes fluttered open. "I need you, Taylor. I want you."

Gritting my teeth against the wave of desire, I

pushed in slightly, her little hitched breaths making me wish I could give up all control.

"Tell me to stop if it's too much," I rasped out, my voice a tight thing I barely recognized.

She shifted her hips and I drew back, making her whimper in protest at my retreat. I reached between us, hoping to make this last, but when she rocked her pelvis up and took me inside her, I groaned and sank to the hilt.

Don't come. Not yet. Make it good for her.

Her tight walls gripped me as I rolled her clit with my fingers and brought her off again.

Pleasure built at the base of my spine, and I was lost to her, ready to fill her with my cum and make sure everyone knew she was mine.

I gritted my teeth as she clenched around me and came again, and I fought off my own orgasm as long as I could. Panic laced the edges of my imminent release. What was I thinking? I was bare, and she could get pregnant.

"God, Taylor."

That was it. Her breathy cry of my name sent me over the edge, and I pulled out, pulsing and shooting ropes of cum onto her belly. With that one gesture, I had marked her as mine.

"Why did you pull out?"

"I didn't want to risk getting you pregnant."

"I can't."

"What do you mean you can't? Are you on the pill?"

"I'm on the pill, and I just finished my period. The chances are microscopic."

"We should still be careful. If anything, I shouldn't have taken you bare. I know enough people who got pregnant while on the pill."

"Don't want you to think I'm trying to trap you." The edge in her voice didn't escape me.

"How could you trap me? I'm already married to you."

"You know that's different."

I stroked her thighs with my palms, loving her soft skin on mine.

"Don't let what my father said get in your head. He's an arse, and you would never try to trap me with a child. That's not how it is between us."

She trailed her fingers through the streaks of my release, and damn if the sight didn't make me twitch.

Then I felt it. All the things I wanted to tell her bubbled up and boiled over. "I know things haven't gone the way I promised they would, but I need you to know there's no one in this world I want more than you. Every day, every minute, every hour. I want to wake up thinking about you. I can't even brush my damn teeth without wondering what you're doing. Even if we weren't married, I would feel the same. I would want you. It broke my heart when you wanted to stop seeing me, and I think all along, this harebrained scheme I had to get out of my contract was really just an excuse. A way for me to be with you."

She reached up and brushed her fingers across my cheekbone. "All you had to do was be this. This kind, caring version of Taylor, the one I met on our first date. That's all I needed."

"I was stupid, but I'm not gonna do that ever again. I don't want to lose you. I don't want to let you go. I want you to be mine. Permanently. I . . . I love you, Becca. I will love you until the very last breath leaves my lungs."

Her eyes widened at my admission, and for a terrible moment she let it hang there, unanswered. But then she gripped my face and pulled my lips to hers. Her tongue delved into my mouth, and she kissed me like I'd never been kissed before. When we broke apart, she nodded, a bright smile on her beautiful face.

"I love you too."

17

BECCA

SOMEHOW, waking up with Taylor wrapped around me this morning was the most perfect thing I had ever felt. Had I really gone all this time without him because I was being stubborn and afraid? I'd wasted so much time letting fear keep me from having what I wanted. He snuggled into me, layering kisses along my shoulder, then did that little biting thing I liked so much where his teeth scraped along my neck.

"Good morning," he murmured against my skin.

"Good morning. Are you ready for the wedding?"

He let out a happy little noise. "Now that I have you for real, I couldn't be more ready to show my family how much I love you."

He rolled me over and tried to kiss me, but I turned my face away. "No!"

"Why not?"

"Morning breath."

"I don't care."

"Well, I do. Hold that thought."

I got up, went into the bathroom, and brushed my teeth. Then, since I was in there, I gave my hair a little finger comb and made sure I didn't look like a bridge troll before coming back out. He sat up, smirking.

"Well, if you're going to brush your teeth, I guess I have to do mine."

"I appreciate your consideration," I said with a laugh.

As he took care of his business, I made myself a cup of coffee and sat by the window so I could stare out at the little town. It was early, but people were already milling around. Shops were opening, the sun shining in the blue sky.

Taylor came out of the bathroom naked and unashamed. Of course he wasn't ashamed; he was absolutely beautiful.

"It looks like it's gonna be a nice day."

"Too bad I'm gonna keep you in bed for most of it."

I grinned. "Is that a promise?"

"Aye, lass. I guaran-fucking-tee it. I have months to make up for."

He leaned over me, careful of the coffee mug,

bracing his hands on either side of the chair, and kissed me long and deep until I was breathless and my eyes fluttered.

"Now back in the bed with you, wife. We have nowhere to be until this afternoon, and I don't want to waste any more time."

Three hours later, try as we might, we could not stay in bed any longer. My stomach growled, deciding it needed to be part of the conversation and announcing it wouldn't be ignored. We dressed and bounded down the stairs into the pub, where we were greeted by the innkeeper with an offer of breakfast, but Taylor declined. Momentarily baffled, I stared at him in shock.

"Hungry. You got that part, right?" I whined, not embarrassed one bit.

Threading our fingers, he leaned in and kissed my temple. "Aye, I got it. But I'm going to take you to one of my favorite bakeries. It's run by a little old woman named Maeve. When I was just a wee lad, she was one of the fae. Old Maeve warned me that if I was sneaky and stole any of her goodies, she would curse me."

I laughed. "And you believed her?"

"Oh, I never mess with the fae. To tell the truth, I'm still a wee bit afraid of her."

"Aren't you precious?"

"I am. You should treasure me forever," he said solemnly.

"I just might do that." He linked our fingers

and tugged me into a bakery, where he ordered each of us a couple of things.

I half expected Maeve to come waddling out, warning us off of falling into any fae circles. But she didn't. Honestly? I was a little disappointed.

Until Taylor took me on a journey through the town and we found the crest of a hill with a bench resting on the top. Together we sat and ate our pastries as he pointed out various locations in the village that were special to him.

"Has it been hard not being back for so long?"

"In a lot of ways, it was easier to just never come back."

"Why?"

He sighed. "Because then I didn't have to long for it so much. But there was a big part of me that was missing. Just didn't realize it." Intertwining our fingers again, he brought my knuckles to his lips. "Thank you for coming with me."

"Your grandfather seems like he's doing pretty well."

"He's not." Taylor frowned, lines bracketing his mouth and deepening between his brows. "He's holding on, pushing through and pretending because he doesn't want anybody to see him looking weak."

"Really?" That tracked, though. Taylor did the same thing. He'd blown out his knee three seasons ago. He hadn't told me, but in my effort to understand my husband better, I had done base-level research. "I guess the apple doesn't fall very far from the tree."

"What do you mean?"

"Well, you do the same thing. And as you said, he's more like your father than your real dad is. It would stand to reason that you've learned how to be because of him."

"You're probably right."

"Is that scar on your knee from when you got injured?" I would have missed it if I hadn't been paying attention, but his shoulders stiffened.

"Aye."

"What happened?"

"It was a stupid accident. Wasn't even on the ice, so luckily, there's no footage of it happening."

"What was it?"

"I'd gone for a run, and a dog had gotten off leash and darted in front of me. So I paused mid-stride, turned quickly, and ruptured my ACL. It was right in the middle of the season. Bad time to get injured. So it was no surprise when I was traded to Seattle."

"Wow. I don't know how I feel about that."

"You don't know how you feel that I had a nearly career-ending injury?"

"No, I . . . that's awful, but also, if it hadn't happened, I wouldn't have met you."

"We were always destined to meet. It would have happened somehow."

"Maybe, but you don't know that. Small changes can result in huge things never coming to pass. They call it the butterfly effect."

"I don't believe in that. I believe in twin flames. And you are mine."

Jesus, the way he could make my heart flutter. "Why were you not this guy when we first started dating? I love this guy."

"You love the other guy too."

"Oh, I love to hate the other guy."

"I don't think you know what hate is. If you did, you'd never have come around to me. That was your body telling you one thing and your head telling you another. I've always been the same guy. You only saw what you wanted to see."

"Because I was scared."

"Because you were scared," he agreed. "But, Becca, I was just as scared. If I hadn't been, I would have laid myself at your feet far sooner than I did."

"Were you really going to just stay on Bainbridge Island with me forever?"

Something flickered in his gaze. Fear? Maybe apprehension? "No, no. We're not allowed to talk about the real world, remember? I've whisked you away to faerie land. This is the only thing we can talk about. Here and now. This moment. No plans for the future. We'll tackle those later, all right?"

"Should we check in? See how things are

going back home?"

"As in check in with my mum?"

"Yeah, make sure she's okay. See if your dad headed your warning or if he went over there anyway."

He pulled this phone out of his pocket and frowned. "Bugger."

"What? What happened?"

"Well, it looks like my relative anonymity is over." He held out his phone, and I saw a message from Ethan Byrne.

Byrne: Does this mean I have to call you your lordship now?

"There was an article posted on Hockey News all about the NHL's secret royal. I'm not even royalty. This is bloody ridiculous."

"Is it going to affect your career?"

"No, but it's going to give me a lot more unwanted attention. And the press loves a scandal. They love anything to do with nobility, even if they don't understand it."

"I guess I don't really understand either, because it's archaic."

He raked a hand through his hair. "It's nothing special. Some fat king gave someone in my family a title a long time ago. It doesn't make us any more special. It just makes us rich. Nobility was the original popular crowd." Heaving a sigh, he grinned at me. "At least it'll be good for business."

"What?"

"I'm nobility, so that makes you, my wife, nobility by default. Everyone will want to come to the bakery owned by a Scottish lady."

"Speaking of, I should check in with Scarlett."

"Haven't you been?"

"Yes, I've texted with her every day."

"And how's the new kitchen?" His eyes sparkled with interest.

"Oh, it's a dream. Really. And so is our staff. We're still selling out every day. And we're booked solid for the next nine months for catering."

"That's fantastic."

"It is, but it's hard to say no when people need us for jobs. I hate telling them I can't fit them in."

"Well, you can't be everything for everyone."

"It's true. But I like to help."

"I know you do. Now go, check in with your sister. I'm not going anywhere."

Snapping a photo of the two of us, I sent the photo to Scarlett, followed by a short text message. She responded instantly.

Scarlett: You look different. You look happy.

Me: I am.

Scarlett: Oh my God. Did you fall in love with him?

Me: Yes?

Scarlett: I knew it. I knew I wasn't going to get rid of that Scottish oaf.

Me: Sorry.

Scarlett: Don't be. Oh, by the way, I got a call from Good Morning America. They want to feature us. I'm sure it has something to do with your fancy duke.

Me: He's not a duke.

Scarlett: It doesn't matter. They want to talk to both of us. Have us on the show and do a demo.

Me: Really? Wow.

Scarlett: Yeah, it's pretty crazy. So when you get back, we'll figure out when we can get over there. Does that sound good?

Me: Yeah.

Scarlett: Okay. Thanks for checking in. I'm over here living vicariously through you.

Me: Maybe you should try living vicariously through you. And by that I mean just living.

Scarlett: Maybe I'll do that. Ethan and Elles are having a party tonight. I wasn't gonna go, but maybe I should.

Me: You definitely should.

Scarlett: Love you. Have fun.

Me: You too.

"That smile is the most beautiful thing I've seen all day," Taylor said, reaching out and tucking a stay lock of hair behind my ear.

"Such a charmer."

"You know that about me. But I will also never lie to you, and that is the honest truth. You're beautiful. Stunning."

"You know, if you're trying to get into my pants, it takes a lot less effort these days."

"Oh, I know. And I'm thankful for it."

"Should we go? I hear there's some sort of nobility getting married today."

"I heard he already got married and this is just a formality."

"True, but I also heard he's rumored to be wearing a kilt to this thing. And I have never gotten to see what's under one before."

"Aye, lass, you have. You were up close and personal with it last night and this morning, and when we get back to the inn, I'll show it to you again."

My thighs clenched tight. Heat pooled low in my belly. "Yes, please."

"Come on then. Time's a-wasting."

"We can't have that. Did I ever tell you about the time I took riding lessons?"

He looked puzzled by my topic deviation. "No."

"It wasn't something I wanted to stick to, but Clara insisted. So I went down to visit her, and my brother-in-law's youngest brother Sutton taught me how to ride."

A low growl left him. "Oh, he did, did he?"

"Oh, yes. He gave me very detailed attention. Made sure I was seated just right. And that I knew how to work my hips."

"Becca, are you trying to wind me up? Because it's working."

"My point is, I never took to horseback riding, but maybe that's because what I really needed was to learn the fine art of beard riding instead."

He grinned wide and dragged a hand over his closely cropped beard. "Oh aye, that is quite a sport. You know, it's been a long time since I've been a participant in having my beard ridden. I think maybe I'd like to take it up again. If you'd like."

"Oh, I'd like. I'd like it very much."

"Let's go, right now."

In a handful of minutes, we were running up the stairs to our room. He slammed the door and threw the lock, and then we were frantic. Tearing at each other's clothes. Kissing so hard my lips would be bruised and swollen. I didn't care. I just wanted him.

And then he laid back on the bed, fully nude, cock hard and jutting. A specimen of perfect masculinity, not a single toxic trait about him. Well, maybe a few. He was a bad boy, after all. With a wicked gleam in his eyes, he licked his lips.

"All right, lass. Your saddle is ready. Come over here and sit on my face."

18

TAYLOR

The wedding party was exactly as I had expected —absolutely over the top and ridiculous. Mum didn't do things by half, and this was a prime example of that. She spared no expense. And thankfully, with the weather being beautiful, we were able to make use of both the outdoor and indoor portions of the space she'd reserved, because the entire bloody town showed up.

All I could think about, however, was being in the room with my beautiful girl and helping her do up the zip of the dress she'd brought for the occasion. It was not quite white—she said it was called ivory—with a plunging back and fitted waist. The bottom of the skirt flared out, and it reminded me of something you might see in the fifties, but sexier. The straps were off her shoulders, nestled just at the curve of each, and I could see every inch of skin from her neck down to the tops of her breasts.

It was painful for me not to take advantage and slide my hand inside the back of her dress so I could touch her, but I held myself back like the grown man I was. At least I wasn't the only one ogling. She was right there with me, taking in my formal kilt wear.

"Fuck, the look in your eyes, hen. I cannae go to this sporting a cockstand."

"You're just going to have to tuck it or tie it down or something," she said with a giggle.

"Tie it down?"

She shrugged, then kissed me. "I'll give it something as a reward later."

A pained groan escaped me, but I pulled it together.

Thankfully I'd been able to get myself under control, and the two of us walked hand in hand onto the grass where the tables were set up.

"Oh my God. Your mom wasn't kidding. It's beautiful.."

"Aye. She's an excellent party planner."

A band was playing, and there was an honest-to-God wedding cake off to one side. Mum rushed up to us, tears in her eyes.

"Oh, look at you. You're so handsome. And you, Becca, you're just a picture. But I have one thing for you. You don't have to wear it if you don't want to." She pulled out a little rosette made of our family's tartan. "I thought you might wear it in your hair."

It was a brilliant idea. It didn't take away from her dress, and it wouldn't be bothersome. I held my breath, waiting to see what Becca would say. Of course, my girl took it graciously and then examined it with a smile.

"That's beautiful. Will you put it in for me?"

She handed it back to Mum, and the photographer circled like a shark who scented blood in the water, snapping photo after photo of my mother placing the bauble in my bride's hair. Then Becca looked at me.

"This is a real wedding," she said with a laugh.

I looked around and then back at my mother. "Aye, it definitely is."

"I hope you two don't mind, but this is the only time I'm going to get to see my boy get married. And his dear granddad will be so happy. Oh, the priest is already here too."

"Priest? We're already married."

"Not in the eyes of God. You may have gotten married legally, but God still should bear witness."

I rolled my eyes, then cut a glance at Becca. "You don't have to do this."

She shook her head. "It's fine. God should get a piece of this action too." Then she rose on her tiptoes and whispered in my ear, "I want to marry you anywhere. Everywhere. Every opportunity. I mean, what does it matter if we've already done it once?"

God, I loved her. I loved her with a fierceness I didn't know was possible. She gave me the same type of feelings I got from scoring the winning goal or stepping onto the ice for the first time for a game. She excited me. She thrilled me. She was full of possibility. But also, she gave me that victorious feeling of validation. The one that said I was worthy. I craved that feeling, and so far, only winning brought the same thing. With her, it was like every moment I was winning.

Fuck, I was a sap. I had tears in my eyes just thinking about how important she was to me. No way I was gonna get through a whole wedding ceremony without tearing my man card up in front of the entire town. You know what? I didn't care.

"All right. Let's do it. Let's get married. In front of God and everyone."

Mum clapped her hands, then squeezed me tight before doing the same to Becca.

In case you were wondering, I was right. I didn't make it through the ceremony without crying like a fucking baby, but I hadn't expected it to be so meaningful. So bloody powerful. Standing there with her in front of me, her gaze only for me as she promised she'd be mine and I did the same for her. It was different now. So different from some rushed courthouse nuptials.

As soon as we kissed and the crowd began cheering, Hamish jumped up on his seat and said, "All right, can we get this party started now? I want cake!"

Harry followed his brother's lead and shouted, "I want to dance!"

Everyone laughed, even my sister, who at first appeared completely mortified.

We danced. We smiled. We shared so many kisses. I taught her a traditional Highland dance, and she joined with the crowd, smiling and laughing the whole time. I hadn't ever seen her this happy, and that made me a little sad. I resolved that from now on, I would do whatever it took to keep her smiling like that.

At the end of the night, as things were winding down, my granddad approached my new bride. He looked more frail than I'd ever seen him, and it sent a pang of grief through me.

"I believe it's my turn, since your father isn't here darlin'."

He handed me his cane and held out a hand to Becca. I didn't miss how it shook. She cut me a worried glance, and I nodded. And then I watched as the woman I loved and the man who was more of a father than anyone had ever been to me danced together in the fading light of day.

We'd come here to make him happy. To give

him something to celebrate at the end of his life. And instead, the old bastard had given me a brand new family without even realizing it. I sat with Becca, watching my nephews each dance with young girls from the town. I looked at her, marveling that I got to call this woman mine.

"Are you happy, love?"

"I'm so happy. Happier than I ever thought possible, actually. I really didn't think love was real."

"I know you didn't."

"But now I know it is."

"Me too."

"So this is real, right?" she asked, her voice hesitant.

"Do you mean to tell me you don't know if it's real, even though you just married me in front of my whole family?"

"I know we were supposed to do that. That was part of the deal."

"Becca, the deal went out the window a long time ago. If you think I'm giving you up ten months from now, you're sorely mistaken. I'm keeping you even when we're old and saggy and..."

"You can't get it up anymore?"

I laughed. "That'll never happen. I'll probably go to my grave with a hard-on."

Her happy giggle nearly did me in. "You know, you're probably right."

"You're mine. I made you a promise 'til death."

"Well, I guess I better legally change my name then."

"You don't have to."

"I want to. I like the way Becca Savage sounds."

"So do I. You know," I whispered, nuzzling her neck. "It's been very hard for me to see you in that dress and not be able to do anything about how much I like it."

"Oh yeah?"

"Yes. Do you think they'd notice if we snuck away?"

"I think that's our prerogative. We are the bride and groom, and it is technically our wedding night. I believe consummation is required to make this legally binding or some archaic rule like that."

"I think you might be right. Should we go back to the room and consummate, wife?"

"Yes, we definitely should, husband."

BECCA

We consummated, all right. We consummated all night long.

When we got back to the hotel, the first time

was fiery and frenzied, but the next few times, it turned reverent, tender, loving. He worshiped me. It was such a strange feeling to know that we were together. Really, truly together. And that I didn't have to worry. He was mine and no one else's. If I had any doubts about his commitment, they were cast aside when he said his vows to me. He was breathtaking in that moment. Then when his grandfather took me out onto the dance floor the way he did and gave me the father-daughter dance I would never have, there was nothing I could have done to stop the tears that spilled out of my eyes as we danced.

Aside from his father, Taylor's family were wonderful, amazing people from what I could tell. I didn't want to leave, but our time here was coming to a close. No matter how much I wanted to stay in our happy little bubble of love, we had to go back to the real world. We had to be adults who returned to our jobs and couldn't just spend every moment of the day basking in each other's arms. Normal life meant obstacles, challenges, and stressful things. Things I knew I could easily end a relationship. I didn't want that for Taylor and me. We'd have to deal with issues like the press, the fans, or life in general, but ignoring it wouldn't be the answer either.

I didn't think anyone went into a marriage hoping it would end. Except for us. That was exactly what we'd done. Given ourselves a solid end date. An out.

I forced myself not to think of all the ways this could go wrong and instead focused on what I had right now. New love, new family. We were in this together. He'd said as much, and I believed him.

I had woken up sticky, and no matter how sexy he said I was, there was a line, and this was one I didn't want to cross. So I got up and padded into the bathroom, leaving him softly snoring in the bed. My muscles were deliciously sore; I was swollen and aching between my thighs, and just the thought of him made me wet.

How could I want him again so soon after the last time? But I did. I was ready to go. Ready for him to take me again. I scrubbed myself clean, the scent of lemongrass and sage waking me up. The bright bite of citrus energized me, and I began humming to myself softly, slowly dancing under the spray of water. As I scrubbed my hair and then rinsed it clean, my eyes closed and my body relaxed. I'd never been this happy. And then large, warm palms cupped my breasts. I groaned as I opened my eyes to see Taylor standing in the shower with me, tattoos running the length of his torso on full display. I wanted to lick them. Trail them with my tongue.

"What are you doing in here?"

"I thought you might want some help."

"I don't think you'll be helpful. I think you'll distract me."

He leaned forward and pressed his forehead to mine. "That's the idea. Let me distract you."

He kissed me. Parting my lips, he slid his tongue inside, and I sucked on it, making him groan. There was nothing I loved more than the sound of his needy groans.

"You were sound asleep when I left."

The rumbled chuckle he let out had my pussy tingling as he spun me around so my back was to his chest. "There was no way I was going to lie there, listening to you singing in the shower, and wait for you to come back."

I moaned as he rolled my nipples, moving me backward so the water didn't hit me in the face.

He was hard and insistent, pressing against the small of my back.

"Haven't you had enough?"

"Not with you. I could never have enough. I want every inch, all the time."

His palms skated down my chest, my belly, my thighs. When he finally got to where I wanted him to be, he grazed my clit with a gentle finger. I groaned and shivered, laying my head back on his powerful chest.

"God, Taylor."

He had me tingling all over.

"Is my wee wife already slick and

ready?" Reaching further, he delved inside. "Oh, aye, she is."

He fucked me with his fingers slowly, grinding his palm against my over-sensitized bundle of nerves.

"Jesus, Taylor, please."

"Oh, lass. I love it when you beg. Now lean forward, part your legs, and grab the ledge. I'm going to fuck you now."

I felt his rigid length notching against my slick entrance. Even after multiple rounds with him, he was still a snug fit. He sank in all the way, his hands holding me by my hips, keeping me steady as the water rained down on us.

"Now rock your hips back into me. Take me . . . take me into you."

His words were stilted and tight as his palms skated along my spine. So I canted back and forth while ragged groans left him, and he whispered, "Fuck, that's hot. Watching your arse while I sink inside you."

I couldn't keep the orgasm at bay. I didn't want to. Especially not when he reached around me and began stroking my swollen clit.

"I love you, Taylor," I said in a broken whisper.

"Fuck, baby, I love you too." We moved together until we were both trembling, and he rasped, "I'm gonna need to pull out."

I didn't want him to. The risk was minuscule. I was on birth control and I knew my cycle.

"No. Fill me up, Taylor. Put your cum where it belongs."

"Christ," he ground out. "Hold on to something."

I already was, but he gripped me hard and began thrusting frantically.

With a pained and pleasured sound, he slammed home, and I felt him pulsing inside me as he came. Filling me up exactly as I'd asked.

The water ran cold by the time we got out, but I didn't care. I was going to stay in this moment with Taylor Savage as long as I possibly could.

19

TAYLOR

I traced Becca's cheek with the tip of my finger as the sunlight crept through the window. I couldn't believe she was really mine. That we'd gone from two people who'd agreed on a mutually beneficial arrangement and become so much more. Truly married. Truly a couple. Truly in love. She was mine in every sense of the word, and I couldn't have asked for more.

"Wake up, hen. It's morning."

She let out a little groan of protest. "No."

"Aye, it is. Don't you hear the birds?"

"That's the nightingale."

I chuckled. "Not even Shakespeare will save you from waking up, my beauty. Come on, out of bed with you. Mum will have breakfast on the table before long. You don't want to end our trip without tasting haggis at least once. She'll never forgive you."

"If you weren't so sexy, I'd throw my shoe at you."

"Would ye?"

"Yes."

"No, you're a Scot now. We don't say yes."

"Aye, then. I'd throw my shoe at your handsome face to shut you up."

Pulling the covers away from her, I groaned at the sight of her soft, curvy frame, barely covered in one of my old uni shirts. Her round arse peeked out from under the hem. No knickers. God, I loved this woman.

I had to touch her. That silky skin, the warmth of her, all of it.

"Mmm," she hummed as she rolled onto her back and parted her thighs. "Maybe I can be persuaded to wake up if this is the prize I get."

"Sit up for me, lovely. Take off that fucking shirt."

My chest tightened as she did what I asked, her full tits drawing my eye immediately. Perfectly teardrop shaped, I loved how they fit in my palms, but most of all, I loved how she moaned when I touched her. I wanted to make her moan here and now.

So I did.

I climbed over her on the bed and slid my hands around her waist, then up until I cupped her breasts. Brushing my thumbs over her pebbled nipples, I leaned in and kissed her once, twice, a third time, until she lay back and welcomed me between her thighs. I was hard as a rock and ready to be inside her. Who was I kidding? I was always ready to be inside her. Bloody hell, I could live there and die happy.

"Your turn to take off the shirt, Mr. Savage."

"My pleasure, lass." I tugged the fabric over my head, exposing the ink I knew she loved so much.

She reached out and ran her fingers along my back, her nails scraping along my spine until she reached the waist of my boxers. The way she stared at me, eyes seeing into my fucking soul, had me fighting the urge to help her as she brought her hands around to the front of my jeans and began working my fly open.

"I need you, Taylor."

"Then you'll have me. You'll have everything you want."

When her hot little hand wrapped around my shaft, I couldn't stop the grunt that escaped me. My lips found hers again as my arms trembled from the effort to hold myself over her as she worked me. In moments, she had me reduced to a creature of primal need, dick leaking pre-cum, balls tight and aching, mind focused on one thing. Filling her.

She shoved the fabric down my thighs, that

one action giving me the freedom I needed to bury myself deep within her. All it took was one long thrust, and I was sheathed in perfect, tight heat.

"Fuck, lass. You're my heaven. I know it."

"I love you," she whispered. "So much."

That snapped me out of the haze of lust and back to the reality between us. This was so much more than fucking. She was mine. My wife. My love. My everything. I cupped her cheek with one hand and drank in every little change in her expression as I rolled my hips with languid movements. The tiny furrow in her brow, the way her lips parted before she released sighs of pleasure, the flicker of frantic energy behind her irises.

My palm drifted from her face to wrap gently around the column of her throat, where I could feel the flutter of her pulse and the way her breath hitched.

"Is this okay?"

"Fuck, yes."

"I love you, too. I never . . ." It was hard to continue when my throat was so tight, my chest about to burst from the overwhelming emotions. "You're the most important thing in the world to me, Becca. I . . ." My words cut off on a groan as she wrapped her thighs around me and pulled me deeper inside her. Her walls fluttered around me, and she cried out, reaching her peak and pulling me right along with her. I spilled my release inside her, not caring that I should have pulled out. Not giving a single damn that I'd never gone bare with anyone before her.

I pulled out, my gaze riveted to the trail of cum that leaked from between her legs. On instinct, I used my fingers to push it back inside her.

"What are you doing?" she asked, a smile in her voice.

"This belongs inside you, and one day, when we're both ready, we're going to make a baby together. I'm just practicing."

She sighed happily. "Well, you are an athlete. Practice makes perfect."

Why is my heart racing like I've been doing speed drills? Are we really talking about this? About starting a family?

"What if I'm not ready when you are?" Tension that hadn't been there before laced her tone.

Fuck. I shouldn't have brought it up. The truth was, I wanted kids, but only with her. "It's okay. It'll happen when it happens. We don't have to talk about it now. We'll get there."

She rolled on her side to face me. "It's a big deal. Life changing. And with my bakery and you traveling during the season . . ."

"Most of it would fall on you. I understand your hesitance."

"It's not just that. We . . . until recently, we hated each other. How can we be talking about having babies?"

I trailed the back of my hand over her arm. "I never hated you."

"I see that now."

"I'm sure about you. That's all that matters to me. I never want us to be apart." Fear curled in my gut. We were going back to the real world after this. To the circumstances that required us to live separate lives.

"Who says we have to?"

"Life. You said it yourself. I'm going back to away games and traveling all the bloody time. You're going back to buttercream and rolling pins and demanding brides."

I hated how needy I sounded, but I hadn't allowed myself to think of this until just now. Not really. I did what I did best, ignored the issue until it either went away or became a problem. My knee gave a throb as if to remind me of the latter.

"My job is more than buttercream and rolling pins."

"You know what I mean. You were in that kitchen all hours of the night, working your pretty little arse off."

"And you will always be practicing or playing."

I tucked a lock of hair behind her ear. "I suppose we'll have to figure out how to make time for each other." She gave me a sweet smile. "Have you talked to Scarlett since the last time? How's the extra staff working out?"

"Not much more than just a text or two each day. It's hard here with the time difference. She seems to be handling it really well, though. The extra staff helps."

That made me proud. I'd done that for her. I'd given her what she needed, but of course, I'd asked for something in return.

"I'm glad."

"It'll take some of the pressure off if we can keep them on."

The idea of easing her burden made my heart swell. "Good. That's good. I just want you to be happy, hen. That's all I've ever wanted."

"You make me happy."

Wrapping her in my arms, I pressed a kiss to the tip of her nose. "You can't know what that means to me."

A harsh banging on the door pulled my attention from my wife and made me wish like hell I'd booked us at the inn for the remainder of our visit. But, after our wedding night, we'd returned to a magically working water heater and my entire family in residence.

"Taylor, if you two don't quit shagging up here, Mum is going to come up here and drag you downstairs by your ear." My sister's voice was strident and annoyed.

Becca erupted into giggles, attempting to get out of bed, but I wasn't having it. I tugged her into me and layered kisses all over her face and neck.

"Mmm, maybe I'll just eat you for breakfast," I murmured against her ear.

"Ugh, I heard that. At least it'll be the two of you giving her wee grandchildren instead of me now."

"Leave me be. We'll be down shortly."

I released my wife and sat up, hating that I had to let her go.

"See that ye do."

Becca leaned close and whispered, "I think she's annoyed with us."

"I don't give a damn."

"At least one of us doesn't." She got up and headed into the loo. "I'm going to take a shower. The last thing I want to do is leave with your mom mad at me."

"Oh, hen, I hate to see you leave, but I do love watching you walk away."

She laughed and closed the door behind her. But every bit of what I'd said was true. She and I would make this work. We had to. I couldn't let anything get between us.

BECCA

With Taylor taking his nephews to the rink for the hockey game he'd promised them, I had time for one last walk through the beautiful fields surrounding his family home. I needed it. Something about this country soothed me, felt like it was welcoming me back to where I belonged. But maybe that was more about the person I was with than the land itself. Taylor had a way of pulling me into his orbit no matter what. Case in point, my impulsive wedding. If he'd been any other man, I would've laughed him right off my porch. But he was charming, and I was a glutton for punishment.

"Are you sure you don't want to come watch them kick my arse?" he asked as I tied my shoes.

He was leaning against the wall across from me in the entryway, his eyes glimmering with mischief.

"As much as I love watching you be an amazing uncle to them, I really want to soak up one more walk out here in Scotland. Who knows when I'll get to come back, you know?"

"I'll bring you back here whenever you want. Hell, we can buy a house here and spend as much time in Scotland as you'd like."

Why did that make me sad? Maybe because I'd never had anything like this before. The ability to simply buy a house in Scotland and jet off to visit whenever I wanted. Money had been tight for my entire life. Clara had scrimped and saved and worked hard to ensure we stayed comfortable. Instead of spending our parents' life insurance, she'd set up accounts for each of us, then worked two jobs to support our family. It had been hard, I was certain, but she never let us see how it affected her. Now, as a business owner, I understood. I wasn't extravagant. I didn't spend money recklessly. Sure, I had fun, went out, and splurged here and there, but I knew it could all go away at any time.

"Hey now, hen, what's that face?" Taylor fell to his knees in front of me and cupped my cheeks with his large hands.

"The money stuff. It's unnerving."

"What are you talking about?"

"I'm not used to it. That's all. I don't like spending your money."

"It's ours now. If you want to spend it, spend it. God knows I make more than anyone should."

My stomach churned. "Do I even want to know how much?"

He chuckled and pressed his forehead to mine. "Probably not. But I want you to have everything. If you need a new car, buy one. If Scarlett wants to move out, help her get a house. What's mine is yours."

"I . . . I just need you to know that even if you didn't have money, I love you. This isn't about what you can buy me. You give me so much more that can't be bought, Taylor."

Fuck, why was I crying?

He brushed the tears away with the pads of his thumbs and kissed me softly. "I know that. Even when it was about the money, I knew you only took it because there wasn't another option. But I'm the luckiest fucking bastard because if you hadn't agreed, I'd be stuck on some reality show like poor Petrov, dating women who have gold digger tattooed on their arses."

Twin Scottish beasties burst through the front door, nearly taking their uncle down as they collided with him.

"Bloody hell, you two, didn't your godforsaken mum teach ye to knock on the door? Ye think you can barrel in here and take over like a couple of English invaders?" He might've sounded angry, but he was very clearly playing with them. "Just because your dad is an Englishman, I'll give ye a pass."

"We were waiting at the gate, but you were taking too long!" Harry—or was it Hamish? —said.

"Fine. Tell this pretty lady to come watch us when she's done with her walk, will ye? She willnae listen to me."

Both boys turned their adorable faces to me. "We're gonna knock out his teeth."

"Oh, please don't. I like them where they are."

"I cannae make any promises, Auntie."

Taylor and I both laughed as he got to his feet. Then, without warning them, he tossed both boys over his shoulders and strode out of the house.

"Come see me, hen. I promise it'll make you love me even more."

I wasn't sure that was possible.

"Love looks good on him." The gentle voice of Taylor's sister reached me from the hallway.

I turned to face her, but she wasn't smiling. "I didn't expect him to..."

"I know. I overheard you. I wasn't trying to eavesdrop, but the boys needed their helmets, and they left them in the game room."

Guilt swirled in my stomach. "It's complicated."

"I'd say it's pretty simple. You needed money for something. He had it. You took advantage and got him to marry you."

"No, that's not exactly how it worked."

"But he did give you money. He's giving you everything he has. Do you even really love him?"

Oh, this was going south real fast. "It was supposed to be temporary. A year. To get him out of a contract and to get my bakery a new kitchen."

"Sounds like you benefited more than he did. Are you going to try and saddle him with a kid too? Get yourself a nice child support check every month?"

She couldn't have hurt me more if she'd hit me. "I'm not pregnant."

"Yet." She wrapped a shawl around her shoulders and held tight. "I've seen this story play out more than once. Handsome athlete, pretty girl, whirlwind romance. You'll use him up and bleed him dry. He deserves more than someone who had to be paid to marry him. You're no better than a whore."

And there it was. The absolute truth. I'd known it all along. Our arrangement was more for my benefit than his, and all I'd done until this trip was fight with him and actively try to pick at him. All he'd wanted was me.

Tears pooled in my eyes, but I forced them back.

"My brother might play at being the cocky arsehole, but he's tender and breakable, Becca. He needs someone who'll care for him, not hurt him. He's been through a lot with our dad. And when I say a lot, I mean it. Please don't break him. If this isn't serious for you, end it now, before you ruin him."

"I love him. I really do."

Sadness flitted across her face. "I hope so. For his sake."

Then she brushed past me, helmets in hand, as she followed in Taylor's wake. I stood there, shaking as my gut churned.

Pulling out my phone, I video called my sister

as soon as I was alone.

Clara answered on the first ring, even though it was the middle of the night.

"Becs, what's wrong?"

I stepped out into the morning mist and wiped my eyes. "I'm in love with him."

"And that's a problem?"

"Yes."

"Why?"

"He's so good, Clara. So, so good. What if I ruin it?"

"You won't. Not if you both keep talking. Don't bottle it up. Tell him when you're afraid, when you're mad, when you're happy. We aren't our parents, Becs."

She hit the nail on the head with that one. "Is that what you and Mav do? You two had an arrangement that started everything. How did you move past the bargain and into reality?"

"Well, it was a long time coming for him. He'd been in love for a long while without admitting it to himself. I was so guarded I couldn't believe he'd ever really want me. But we fell into the self-doubt pitfalls of our own baggage. It almost ruined everything, remember?"

I thought back to a very similar phone call she and I had when she was pregnant and the two of them had almost called it quits. "But you went and told him how you felt."

"I was honest with him. I didn't let him self-sabotage. And we made each other promise never to hold our cards to our chests again."

I swiped the tear off my cheek as I continued walking. "I'm afraid to need him like Mom needed Dad. They were so bad for each other."

"It's okay to need people. I need Mav every day, and he needs me. Don't let that shut you down. Let him love you. You deserve it."

Nodding, I took a shuddering breath, then let it out with a shaky sigh. "God, sorry to have a complete breakdown on you in the middle of the night."

"It's okay. I was up anyway. Morning sickness is a misnomer, by the way."

"Wait, what? You're pregnant again?"

She grinned. "Eight weeks. Mav is insufferably proud of himself."

"That's so great. Quinn needs a little brother or sister to boss around."

A wail filtered through the phone, pulling my sister's attention from the screen. "Speaking of. I gotta go. I love you, Becs. You're going to be fine. I promise."

"Love you too. Thank you."

As soon as we hung up, I shoved my phone in my back pocket and strode toward the rink. She was right. No matter how we got here, Taylor and I were meant to be. We loved each other, and I wasn't going to let anything get in the way of that. Not even my own fears.

20

TAYLOR

My beautiful wife sighed and rolled over in our bed, her long hair fanned across the pillow, blankets exposing most of her back and the top of her arse. Reaching out, I pulled the duvet up to cover her, not wanting her to be cold this early in the morning.

The sky was the deep blue of approaching dawn, not yet light enough for more color to streak across the horizon. I knew I should have tried to sleep longer, but I couldn't. I had a lot to think about. Plans to make. A life to build piece by piece.

Securing my knee brace, I stretched my leg and nodded, something loosening in my chest when I felt nothing more than the usual tightness around the scar. Thank fuck. I'd really thought I'd hurt myself when Hamish took me out on the ice yesterday. The flight home had been hell.

"What are you doing?"

"I'm going for a run. I can't sleep."

"Fucking jet lag," she grumbled. "What time is it?"

"4:15. I'll be back before you know it." I sat on the edge of the bed and ran my fingers across her cheek.

"Be careful."

Leaning down, I kissed her temple before standing and popping my earbuds in. "Go back to sleep, hen. Then I can wake you properly when I get home."

"Mmm, promises, promises."

I winked at her as I left, my cock responding to the idea too.

The bite of the chilly morning air hit my cheeks as I stepped outside into the quiet neighborhood.

My feet hit the pavement as I ran down the darkened sidewalk, music blaring in my ears, the beat thumping through me and keeping my pace steady. I timed my breaths, working to keep myself controlled, but all I really wanted was to get home and be done with this so I could shower and wrap up in Becca.

We'd only been back for twenty-four hours, but I already felt like I was losing her to normal life, to the pressure of her business and my job and the expectations of everyone else around us. Just as I had feared. I took the corner and made my way down the long hill leading to the main street downtown. None of the businesses were open yet, as it was fucking early, but it gave me a chance to run by the bakery and see what my wife and her sister had built together.

Surprisingly, the lights were on, and I could hear music coming out of the open window. Scarlett's old red Honda Civic was parked around the side in the alley. She and I hadn't really had much chance to get to know each other. So far, her only impressions of me were probably ones I'd rather not know about. She didn't hate me, but she was suspicious. And I didn't blame her. I hadn't proven myself to be worthy of her sister. But I sure as hell was going to try.

I knocked on the back door, but she didn't hear me. So I tried the handle, and it opened easily. Walking in, I called out, "Scarlett? Are you there?"

I found her hunched over the toilet in the small washroom, puking her guts out.

"Oh my God. Are you all right, lass?"

Her shoulders sagged, and she rested her forehead on her arm, sighing in defeat.

"What are you doing here?"

"What are you doing here? I'm relatively sure you shouldn't be baking a damn thing if you're vomiting."

"I'm fine. Leave me alone."

"What do you mean, you're fine? You were puking your guts out. Being sick all over the bathroom."

"I made it to the toilet this time."

"Where were you last time?"

"The garbage bin."

"Scarlett, why are you here? You should be resting. You're sick."

"I'm not sick."

"Yes, you are. By the look of you, I would say you're quite ill. Let me drive you home."

"No, you don't need to."

"I'm not going to let my new sister-in-law drive herself home sick and shaking. You're pale. Your skin is all clammy. You should be in bed."

"It'll pass."

"Will it?"

"Yes, it will."

"Scarlett, what's going on?"

She got to her feet, flushed the toilet, then washed her hands. I snagged a cup of water for her and handed it over. After rinsing out her mouth and then taking a hearty gulp of the water, she leveled her gaze on me.

"You cannot tell anyone, and by anyone, I mean my sisters or any of your teammates."

"What are you going to tell me?" Fuck, I was worried. Very worried I was going to be harboring a secret I shouldn't be keeping. "You're not knocked up, are you? You're a virgin. That's sort of your thing."

She closed her eyes, tilted her head up, and took a long, deep breath.

"Scarlett, the virgin." She sighed. "Scarlett, the idiot virgin who got knocked up on her very first try."

Tears welled in her eyes before trailing down her cheeks almost immediately.

"I was just kidding. You're not really . . ."

"Yes. Really. I'm such an idiot."

"Oh, don't cry, lass."

I didn't know what to do. So I did the only thing I could think of—step forward, wrap her in my arms, and hold her against my chest as she cried.

"Who?" I mostly growled.

She shook her head. "I don't want to say."

"Who?" I insisted.

"Trick."

I stiffened. "Patrick, Trick? Patrick Huston?"

My teammate had knocked up my sister-in-law? She had to be kidding me.

"What? I didn't know the two of you were—"

"We weren't. And we aren't. And I don't know if I'm going to tell him, so please don't mention it. I don't know what I'm going to do."

"You . . . you had a one-night stand with Trick?"

"Yes. I just wanted to not be the virgin

anymore. And we were at a party at Big Deck's house, and everyone was drinking, and Trick was so sweet. We danced, and he kissed me, then I invited him home for another drink. He came with me all the way out here, and then one thing led to another and..."

"I'm going to kill him."

"No, don't kill him."

"He didn't even use protection. The bleeding idiot."

"He did. It broke. And I was on the pill, so I told him it would be fine. Except I don't know what happened. It wasn't supposed to happen, but it happened. God, I'm so stupid."

"No, you're not stupid. Things like this happen. It'll be all right. We'll take care of you."

She broke out of my hold. "I don't want you to take care of me. Everyone's been taking care of me my whole life. I'm the little sister who never gets anything right. Who has to rely on her big sisters to take care of her. I will figure this out. But you can't tell anyone."

"Scarlett, this isn't something I can keep from Becca."

She sighed. "So you're that guy? The good guy now? I thought you were the liar. The cocky asshole. Just when I need you to be a dick, you grow a conscience."

"Becca deserves to know."

"No, she doesn't. It's my decision who to tell and when to tell them."

She had a point. I was not involved in the least. She was the one who should tell whoever she wanted.

"You don't have to do this by yourself. You should tell your sister. She won't shame you. It could have just as easily been her."

That thought sent a thrill through me. She stared at me. Her face was so like her sister's, but there was fear in her eyes, and her lower lip trembled. Then she went a little green, and I backed away as fast as possible as she ran for the toilet.

There must have been something on the slick floor because my foot slipped out from under me, and as I heard her emptying the contents of her stomach once more, I twisted and reached to grab hold of the counter.

Something in my knee snapped. I fell to the ground. Pain. Fucking pain I was all too acquainted with radiated from my knee straight through to my heart.

"Fucking hell," I groaned, sitting up and tentatively touching my knee.

I was going to be sick right along with Scarlett. I tried to stand, but it hurt too badly.

"Scarlett," I called out, my voice thick with pain.

She came running, her cheeks red, eyes still streaming with tears.

"Oh my God, what happened?"

"It's my knee. Fuck, my fucking knee."

I glanced down at the floor and saw I had inadvertently stepped in a dollop of rainbow buttercream. "Can you help me up?"

She did, but as soon as I tried to put weight on my injured leg, I nearly passed out from the blinding pain.

"Jesus Christ. Call Becca. I need her."

"What?"

"I said, call fucking Becca."

The only person I wanted to see right now was my wife, because I knew what this meant. This was probably the end of my career. This meant I'd be lost with nothing to do. No identity. Or even worse. I'd be benched, and I'd sit and waste away while younger, more fit men played. I would lose her if that happened. I couldn't lose her.

21

TAYLOR

My phone rang as I sat on the back porch, my knee throbbing right along with my head. I was so tired of hurting. This time around, my recovery was slower, but I didn't want to take the meds. I didn't want to risk becoming dependent on them, even though Becca reminded me time and again that if I couldn't sleep, my body wouldn't heal. I'd seen the ugly side of painkillers far too many times. I didn't want to get up close and personal with it.

"You know, answering the phone is part of the equation here, Hook." Even Becca's teasing use of my nickname didn't make me smile.

My wife came out next to me and placed a steaming mug of tea on the small table between the two chairs. The phone continued to buzz, but

I didn't want to talk to anyone right now. Least of all Ethan Byrne.

"You have to talk to them. They're just checking on you."

"Why, so I can tell them I'm an old, wrung-out, useless teammate? That I might never get better? That this was probably the end of my career? Hell, I should probably just move back to Scotland and be done with it."

"You can't be serious."

"I am. It's that or get traded or benched. If I can't skate with as much power for as long as I used to once the season starts, I'm no good to them. This was our first winning season. This team is building something. I can't bring them down. They'll let me go, make a trade with a different team for someone they can build up."

"Retiring is pretty extreme. The doctor said—"

I scoffed. "The doctor said a lot of things."

He told me I should be on my feet in six weeks, that I'd likely regain full range of mobility *if* I was careful. That was a big difference from the last time. The last time they told me I would be one-hundred percent, that I could skate like nothing had ever happened. But that had been years ago. And I was an older man now.

I sighed, my anger and frustration landing squarely on her shoulders. "Quit harping on me. Let me deal with this on my own."

"We're married. You don't deal with anything on your own anymore. That's what I'm here for. Sickness and in health, right?"

"We never said those vows."

She sucked in a tight breath, then set her jaw and trained her attention out into the backyard. My phone rang again, and she picked it up before I could ignore it.

"Hello?" she said, answering the call.

"Becca, hey there, darlin', this is a surprise. I was calling your husband." Maverick Wilde's voice rumbled through the line as she put it on speaker.

"Well, my husband is being a stubborn ass. What do you need?"

"I was just checking in on him. Wanted to make sure he was doing okay. See if he needed anything."

She glanced at me, but I kept my lips tightly shut and shook my head.

"He says no. But I think he's lying."

Bloody hell, this was the last thing I needed. Someone babying me, treating me like I was an invalid.

"Well, if I know anything about Taylor, it's that he's got grit. Tell him I said to listen to the doctor. Take his meds."

How did he know I wasn't taking my meds? Was she talking to him about me behind my back? Was she sharing personal shit? Fuck. I couldn't have the team's owner knowing this was going on.

"I'm working on him. He's resting right now. Doing a good job of staying off his knee, but his first physical therapy appointment is tomorrow. So we'll see how that goes. I'll keep you posted."

No, she fucking would not.

"Do you and Clara want to come over for dinner?" she continued, staring me down.

I glanced at myself. Surely she didn't mean tonight. I was minging. I hadn't showered in days. Fuck.

"When?"

"I was thinking tonight, if it's not too short notice."

How the hell did she think she'd get away with not even asking me?

"I think we can make that work. We can get a babysitter or—"

"No! Bring Quinn with you. I haven't snuggled my niece in a long time. I'll ask Scarlett to come too."

My stomach churned. Scarlett. Her sister who burdened me with a secret she still hadn't mentioned. Her pregnancy. I'm sure I would have heard about it by now if she had.

"Oh yeah, that'd be great. Clara hasn't been able to get a hold of her. You guys must be busy."

"Yeah, we are. Lots of parties and orders to cater."

"Well, that's good news."

"It is. It's a good problem to have. I like staying busy, you know."

"So does that sister of yours I'm married to. It's so hard to get her to take a break. Dinner will be nice tonight."

"Sounds good. I'll see you guys around six."

"I'll let Clara know. Tell Taylor we're all thinking about him, okay? And that if he needs anything, all he has to do is ask."

"I will. I've got you on speaker. He heard you."

"I mean it, Taylor."

I grunted in response, then waited as she hung up the phone.

"You shouldn't be answering my phone, lass."

"Why not? You sure weren't."

"Because it's my phone. What if it had been a personal call?"

"From who? Your other girlfriend, your secret wife? A hot nurse?"

I grumbled. "You know you're the only one for me."

"Oh, I know. Even though you are a terrible patient and grumpy to boot. Is this what you're going to be like when you're old?"

That made a slight quirk lift one side of my mouth. "God willing."

"I guess it's good I'm getting a glimpse of it now so I can prepare myself for thirty years in the future."

"I'm not that old. Do you really think that when I'm in my fifties I'm going to be a crotchety old man?"

"If the shoe fits."

"I'm going to get you for that, Tink."

"I'd like to see you try. You are slow."

"I'm injured."

"Doesn't matter. That gives me the high ground."

"Just to wait until I'm able to get my revenge."

"I look forward to it," she said, flouncing off, pleased as punch that she'd made me play with her.

A few hours later, I'd managed to shower slowly and carefully with my wife's help like I was a hundred years old. I dressed in a pair of gym shorts and a Cyclones T-shirt before I hobbled out of the downstairs guest room. I found Becca standing with Clara, a glass of wine in her hand and her baby niece on one hip.

She was the most beautiful thing I'd ever seen. Watching her hold that little girl, just as natural as can be, as she smiled and laughed with her older sister sent a hum of possibility through me.

Would it really be so bad if I retired? We could have a couple of kids, build a life here. I could help her with her business if she'd let me. My girl was staunchly independent.

"Savage. How are you doing, man? It's good to

see you," Mav said as he clapped me on the shoulder. "Can I grab you beer?"

"No thanks. It's not supposed to drink while I'm on pain meds."

"Oh, right. Shit. Sorry. I didn't even think about that. My brother Luke broke his leg after he was thrown from a horse. I should have remembered he couldn't drink until those pain meds were done."

"So you really are a full-blooded cowboy?"

I hadn't really spent much time with my brother-in-law. It felt weird, him being the boss, holding my livelihood in his hands, but I knew the gist of his family. A lot of men claimed to be cowboys, wore the hats and boots and big belt buckles, but hadn't ever ridden a horse. Hell, some even owned ranches they never stepped foot on. But Maverick wasn't one of them.

"Yep, I really am one-hundred percent Grade A certified."

"What's that like?"

"What's what like?"

"Being a cowboy. I've only ever seen it in TV and movies."

"I guess you didn't get a good look at the ranch when y'all came over for the after-game party, did you? Sunrise is a pretty special place. There's a lot of us, and we've sort of built a community. Small towns are like that."

That made me think of Scotland and all the

people back home who celebrated my wedding to Becca. There was so much joy.

"You should come out sometime when we're not with the team. Bring Becca. You guys can stay at the ranch and ride whenever you want. Watch the sunsets. That's my favorite part."

"The sunsets?"

"Yeah. Nothing like a Montana sunset."

I smiled, thinking of the one sunset I saw at Wilde Horse Ranch. All I'd been focused on was missing Becca at the time. "I'll see if I can steal her away for a weekend once I'm back on my feet."

"Yeah, how's that going? You're standing, so that's better than I thought it would be."

To tell the truth, I wasn't putting any weight on my knee, but he didn't need to know that.

"I'm getting there. I should be ready to go for the season."

"I wanted to talk to you about that." Mav's jaw clenched.

Bollocks. Here it came. They were gonna get rid of me. I could tell by the look in his eyes, the nerves flashing in his expression. I was surprised he was gonna tell me to my face instead of just arranging the deal and sending it to my agent, who had also been calling me every day.

I swallowed past the thick lump in my throat. "Excuse me, I better see if Becca needs any help."

Hobbling across the deck, I reached my wife,

and I couldn't help but smile as Quinn turned her gaze on me and let out a squeal. Clara placed her hand on her already swelling middle.

"She seems to really like her uncle Taylor," Clara said.

"Kids just love him." Becca beamed.

"I have no idea why."

"Probably because you're a big kid at heart."

Was that a good thing? I wasn't sure.

"How are you feeling?" Becca asked. "Do you need a chair?"

She grabbed my shoulder, but I shrugged out of her hold. "I'm fine, woman. Leave me alone. Stop fawning all over me."

The look on her face made me feel like an arsehole. And I was. All she was trying to do was help me because I was hurt.

"I just came over to ask if you need any help."

"No, I got it. I know how to walk."

I was fucking all this up, and I knew it, but as the night wore on and I watched her with her family—grateful as hell that Scarlett did not show up—something hit me that I hadn't wanted to admit until now. Becca Barnes didn't need me for anything. In fact, all I was going to do was break her heart. If I got traded, she'd have to give it everything up to stay with me, and then she'd resent me forever. There was only one thing I could do: separate myself from the woman I loved so she could have the success she truly deserved.

I'd let her go before we got in so deep there was no way we could get out, and eventually, she'd move on. I'd be nothing but a blip on her radar, a mistake she made one summer. These people loved her. They'd take care of her. They'd give her everything she needed, all the support, and I would move on, start over on another team, play for five more years if I was lucky. And then move home to Scotland, as far away as I could get from the woman who owned my heart. Because loving her meant letting her go.

BECCA

Three weeks into Taylor's recovery, he had only pulled away from me more. He didn't want my help. He didn't want to talk to me, and every time he got a phone call from his agent or anybody on the team, he shut down. Something bad was happening with him, and I couldn't tell what it was. He was slipping through my fingers, and I had no way of stopping it.

I stared down at the macarons I was busy filling, a custom order for a wedding that I'd gotten up extra early to work on because there was nothing worse than a stale macaron. It was a travesty when it happened. I had hoped that focusing on creating this delicate confection would help me stop obsessing over how to help my husband. So far, nothing had done the trick.

The back door opened, and Scarlett trudged inside, her hair haphazardly thrown on top of her head in a messy bun, cheeks puffy and flushed, skin coated in a sheen of sweat, even though it was still chilly in the morning.

"You look like hell," I said before swirling a perfect amount of filling onto the next cookie.

"Gee, thanks. Not all of us can roll out of bed and look fresh as a fucking daisy."

"God, you're cranky. What's wrong?"

"Nothing. I'm just not feeling good."

"You should go to the doctor. You've been fighting this for a long time."

"I'm not sick. I told you, I'm fine."

"Still. It could be something more serious."

"I know. I'll make an appointment."

"Okay."

"Will that make you feel better?"

"Yes, it would. I already have one person refusing help in my life. I don't need another."

As I finished up the last macaron on the tray, I set the piping bag aside and removed my gloves before pouring myself a fresh cup of coffee.

"I can't believe you're here this early," she said, fighting a yawn. "What time did you wake up?"

"Three, though I never really went to sleep. I can't sleep without Taylor."

"Wow. How did you go from independent badass who wanted nothing to do with him to this?"

"What do you mean, this?"

"You can't sleep without him."

I sighed. "It's different now. I want him with me. I want to know he's all right and have the comfort of his arms whenever I need them. I love him. That means I want him around all the time."

"Sure."

"Don't sure me."

"I just think it's a little crazy. Like, you barely know the guy. You spent one night with him and suddenly it's all hearts and flowers and everyone's in love, and you're gonna be together forever, blah, blah, blah, and then suddenly it's not that anymore, and he doesn't even return your calls, and then starts ghosting you, even when you have a problem that you need his help with. And I just can't really—"

"Scarlett, what are you talking about?"

"Nothing."

"Are you seeing someone?"

"No. I was seeing someone just for a little bit. It turned out badly. I'm sorry. It's just hard to see you so happy with him, and loving him, and him loving you and... you two are so disgustingly happy. Then

Mav and Clara are over there, adding to their brood and smiling at each other all the time. I'm here alone, nobody wants to be with me, and I hate it."

I stared on in horror as my little sister burst into tears.

"Oh my God, Scarlett. Why didn't you tell me this was going on?"

"There's nothing to tell. And besides, you'd just tell me you told me so anyway."

"What do you mean?"

She sighed. "I can't believe he didn't tell you. That asshole surprised me. I thought he'd do my dirty work for me."

"What are you talking about?"

"I'm pregnant. Okay?"

"You're what?"

Flailing in exasperation, she said, "Knocked up. Up the duff. Preggo. Expecting. You know, having a baby?"

"Scarlett, but . . . you're a . . . virgin." I knew the moment the shocked words escaped my lips that had been the wrong thing to say.

She stared at me like I was an absolute idiot.

"Obviously not anymore."

"Who?"

"It doesn't matter. I'm not talking to him ever again."

"How far along are you?"

"I don't really know yet. No, that's a lie. I

know exactly when it happened. I think I'm about eight weeks."

"Have you been to the doctor?"

"No. I'm still trying to decide what I want to do."

"Sure. What do you want to do?"

"I'm not sure. I wasn't expecting this. Part of me it's always wanted to be a mom, but . . . I just . . . it's not the right time. My life is kind of a mess. And we're so busy . . ."

I crossed the floor and took her hands in mine, staring into her eyes. "Listen to me. I'm here, in your corner. No matter what decision you make. If you want to have this baby, I will be there by your side, holding your hand the entire way no matter what."

"And if I don't?"

I swallowed my throat dry, my stomach in knots because she was facing an impossible choice. There was no way in hell I was going to judge her for it.

"If you don't want to do this, you don't have to. I will help you make the appointment. I will take you to that clinic. I will stay with you. No one's going to abandon you for making a decision like that, and we're not going to judge you. This is a life-changing moment for you. I just need you to know that no matter which way you go, I'm here for you and I support you."

She blinked as tears ran down her cheeks. "Okay, thanks. I really need to think about it."

"Okay. If you want to come over and just sit on the deck and think about it with me, you can."

She wrapped her arms around me and hugged me like she used to when she was little, with her whole body suctioned to me like a little octopus.

"You really don't want to tell me who it was?"

"No. No, I really don't."

"Was it at least your choice?"

"Yes. It was my stupid choice."

"Okay. Was it good?"

She laughed through her tears. "So good. Really, really good. Like the forever kind of good, which of course is stupid. Forever doesn't exist with fuckboys like that one. I should have known that."

"I just—"

"No. I don't want to talk about it anymore. Can we just decorate some fucking macarons, please? I'm finally not feeling sick this morning, and I'd really like to do something normal that doesn't involve me hanging my head in the toilet."

"Sure."

She washed her hands and I did the same, then we went back to filling the cookies. Each of us with our own tray. Mine were salted caramel chocolate, and she had blueberry cream with a brush of gold dust on the top. As I swirled the filling around onto what seemed like my millionth cookie of the day, something occurred to me.

"You said he didn't tell me. Did Taylor know about this? You told him, but you didn't tell me."

Her shoulders slumped. "It wasn't like that. Don't get mad at him."

I couldn't help it, though. It was a big secret to keep from me. It hurt. "I don't know why you wouldn't tell me."

"I wasn't gonna tell anyone. But he came in and caught me barfing, and it just sort of slipped out. Then he stepped in the buttercream, and he fell and hurt his knee. He promised he wouldn't tell you, and I kind of threatened him. I wasn't ready for anybody to know. I was so embarrassed."

Maybe that's why he's been so distant, because he had a secret from me. He was hurting and dealing with his injury, but also, he was trying to keep it close to his chest so he didn't break Scarlett's confidence.

"Promise you won't be mad at him. I swear, I forced him to agree. He wanted to tell you. I think probably if he hadn't hurt himself, he would have."

"I am not mad at him, but it makes a lot of sense now."

"What does?"

"His decisions."

"What do you mean?"

"I mean, the choice he made to keep me away while he's recovering is probably to do with this. So it's actually really helpful to know."

"Yes, probably you're right. And men are so funny about being hurt. They don't like their precious masculinity to be threatened."

"I'm just gonna call and check in on him."

"Okay. Sure. I'll just be here. Filling macarons until the day I die."

Shaking my head at her dramatics, I grabbed my phone and walked out back, taking my coffee with me before sitting on the small chair at the cafe table we had for breaks during good weather.

He was a lion with a thorn in his paw. That made so much more sense, and it lifted a weight off me. I didn't like feeling as though we were drifting apart, but as I brought my phone up to my face so I could video chat with him, notification after notification popped up on my screen. Text messages from Clara, from Elles. Plus Google alerts about my husband and my business, and my stomach churned.

I hadn't expected to ever see these. My business was rarely in the news. But I set it up a long time ago because I wanted to know when people were talking about us or when news outlets maybe mentioned us. Our social media accounts, up until recently, had been deader than a doornail. But when I married Taylor Savage, things changed. It was a slow trickle. The more I was photographed with him, the more the store was mentioned.

We didn't get looky-loos or clout chasers coming into the shop, but it gave us more attention and more business. Usually, the alerts were little, like a mention of Taylor Savage and his wife, blah, blah, blah, or some such nonsense. But today, the first news article I selected was one I wished I could put away and never look at again. A picture of my husband with his knee brace on, a baseball cap covering his head, the brim pulled down low as he walked out of his attorney's office with a manila folder in his hands.

The headline read, **Trouble in Paradise for the Scottish Bad Boy and His Bride? Taylor Savage Visits High-Powered Divorce Attorney.**

Now I was the one who was going to put her head in the toilet. I didn't even know he was going anywhere today. There had been no indication that this was on the horizon. It had only been a few months, and I thought we were happy.

A text came through from Elles.

Elles: It's going to be okay. I'm gonna kill him. But it's going to be okay. This isn't going to hurt the business. You know what they say? No publicity is bad publicity.

I typed back a quick message.

Me: What are you talking about?

But then she sent me the article.

Hockey's Bad Boy Narrowly Escapes Gold Digger's Plot.

I shouldn't have read it. But I did. And it made me sick. It all came through in a blur. Pictures of us were analyzed for body language. They picked me apart, showing how hesitant I was to touch my husband. How I distanced myself from him at every event we went to and how successful my new business was now that my husband had given me his money. There was no mention of our agreement, just that Taylor confirmed his father's report that he'd funded the expansion of our bakery, and then we got married on a whim. The thing that hurt the most was his quote. "No one expects something like this to last."

I hadn't expected it to last. Not until I fell in love with him. And now? Now I was the stupid one.

My phone rang. Taylor calling. Why even bother?

I answered, frantically swiping my tears away as I realized it was a video call. And there he was, wearing that fucking hat.

"Tink? Are you all right?"

"What do you think?"

"I'm sorry. This got out of hand."

"I'll say. You know, if you weren't happy, you

could have just told me. You didn't have to go and draw up divorce papers."

"You don't understand what's going on."

"Yeah, I do. You're done with me. You're moving on. You've decided nothing lasts forever. Right? You didn't expect this to last."

"I didn't expect it to last, and things are changing so fast. It wouldn't be fair to you for me not to prepare."

"Not to prepare? God, Taylor. I'm not even mad at you. I just feel like an idiot. They're leaving one-star reviews of the bakery online. All your little fangirls. They're coming for me because I hurt their precious bad boy. Did you know that?"

"No. Why?"

"Have you seen the articles? The ones you gave them quotes for? I'm a gold-digging bitch. I knew this was a bad idea."

"I didn't . . . they took those quotes out of context."

"Whatever. It's done. I'll sign anything you want. Just be gone before I get home. I don't want to see you."

"I'm not leaving."

"Why not? You clearly checked out of this relationship weeks ago. Go back to Seattle. Go back to your fucking penthouse and get back on the app. Find yourself some other willing woman. I'm done."

"Hen—"

"I'll pay you back every cent you gave me for this since I'm not holding up our end of the bargain."

"Please, Becca."

"Taylor, do yourself a favor. Quit while you're ahead. I know it's a novel concept for you, but I'm trying to be the civil one here. Get out of the house and get out of my life so I can start getting over you."

My heart shattered as I bled out right there on the back porch of the bakery I loved so much.

22

TAYLOR

It had been three days since I had heard from my wife. Three bloody days of torture because I'd gone and fallen in love with her and then let my fears send me running. Because even though I didn't leave her, I closed myself off and basically abandoned her.

How could I have been such a fool to think I wouldn't do something stupid and fuck all of this up? Of course she'd leave. Everyone fucking left. And I deserved it because I hadn't even had the foresight to think about what asking her to move would do to her. She had a career, a business, and a family she loved. She couldn't simply pick up and move because I needed to. But in my defense, this wasn't supposed to be anything more than a one-year arrangement between us. How was I supposed to know I wouldn't be able to live without her?

So here I was. Stuck between a rock and the fucking hardest place I've ever experienced.

"What is wrong with you? What is wrong with him?" Petrov asked me, and then Trick immediately after when I didn't respond.

Coming to stand near me on Byrne's ridiculously huge deck, my teammate cocked one thick eyebrow as he sized me up. The sun was just about to dip below the horizon, casting the early summer sky in hues of pinks and purples.

"You can't tell me you didn't hear the news," Trick said. "Were you not paying any attention? There's serious talk of trading Savage."

"What? Why? Where would you go?"

I couldn't lie; his concern was something I really needed right now. I was an arsehole to them on the best of days, so to know they didn't want me to leave meant a lot.

"Vegas," I grumbled.

"No, I didn't know that. I'm sorry. I thought for sure they'd renew your contract."

"Yeah, well, nothing's set in stone."

I took a long pull of my whiskey, relishing the burn.

"Where's your wife tonight?"

"How should I know?"

"You don't know? You haven't been married for that long."

"Three months," I recited on reflex.

God, had it really been three months? That's all it had taken for me to fall in love with Becca. But I guess I'd been falling in love with her for the better part of a year.

"I think she's had enough. She'll be moving on before I leave."

"No." Petrov seemed genuinely upset, which was surprising. I always thought the big guy hated me.

"What do you care?"

"What do I care? Love is the most important thing there is. Why do you think they write songs about it? Or books, movies, TV shows?"

"I should just let her go," I said, downing my drink.

Petrov smacked me hard on the shoulder. Hard enough that I winced.

"Careful with the goods, man. I'm not wearing padding."

"Wake up and look at what's in front of you."

"What are you talking about?"

"Your whole life hangs in the balance, and you're going to let her go?"

"It wasn't supposed to get this far. I wasn't supposed to fall in love with her."

"You married her. Of course you were supposed to fall in love."

"We made a bargain. One year and then we'd part as friends. That was the gist of it anyway."

"Did you really think you'd be able to just be friends with her?" Trick asked, after staying silent and soaking all of this up.

He and I had our own issues. I wasn't able to mention it yet, but we'd have our moment as soon as Scarlett gave me the go-ahead.

"I don't know. I tricked myself, I guess."

"And now? Do you really think you're going to be happy without her?" Petrov leaned against the deck next to me.

"She is the most important person in my life. But if I'm traded..."

"What if you're not?"

The guys all knew about Becca's bakery. They frequently ordered from her and had gifts shipped to their families for special occasions.

"Do you know she won't leave the bakery behind? Does she think you're asking her to?"

"If I get traded, I don't have an option. I have to go. We would have to leave, and she'd lose everything she's built."

"And what if you don't get traded? What if you stay here for the rest of your career? You could retire here, and she wouldn't have to give up anything." Petrov downed his drink and let out a satisfied sound. "Perfect solution."

"That's a great idea in theory, but we know it doesn't work that way. I haven't been playing at my best since I aggravated my knee. This team is growing. They're going to trade me, if not this time, soon. I should have thought about that more than just in passing. But I was selfish. I was too focused on my own bullshit to see that involving her in this with me was asking too much."

"She loves you," Petrov insisted.

"She did. Don't know about now."

Of course Byrne's wife Elles, who was Becca's best friend, decided now was the right time to insert herself into the conversation.

"She does love you, Taylor. What you did to her was a real dick move."

"Wait, what did you do?" Petrov asked, his dark brows pulling together.

"He leaked their arrangement to the press."

"No, that was not me. That was my giant twat of a father."

"Your dad did that?" Trick asked. "Do you need another drink?"

"Actually now that you mention it, I could use one."

"Why would he do that?" Elles questioned, still angry but softer now.

"Because he's an arsehole. Do you need more reasons?"

"I guess not. So he told the press you two had made a deal?"

"Aye, and she was very hurt."

"How did he know?"

"I shared it with my sister because the lass is more intuitive than she has a right to be."

"So you shared it with your sister, and your sister then shared it with your father."

"Aye, who then sold our story to the tabloids."

"You made her the center of attention in a very bad way. What did she do?"

"She kicked me out, broke my fucking heart. I deserved it. Wouldn't you do the same thing?"

Elles shifted back and forth uncomfortably. "Yes, I would."

"I humiliated her. I didn't want that to happen. Tell me how to fix this, Elles."

"This isn't about the story. It's the fact that you told your sister that she was basically nothing more than a bargain."

"What are you talking about? I never said that."

"That's not what she told me. She said on your last day there, your sister had some choice words for her right before he left for the airport. She warned her, in no uncertain terms, that if Becca was just using you for fame, she would never forgive her. And then, what happens after the two of you have a fight?"

I sighed and ran my hand over my face. "The story breaks."

"The story breaks, and you went to see a divorce attorney. So I don't know if it was your dad or her, but what I do know is you broke my friend's heart, and now she's alone, pregnant, and she doesn't know what to do because her husband is too much of a baby to just talk to her."

My stomach lurched as I ignored the bit about a divorce attorney. I could deal with that later. There was another very important word she'd dropped like a bomb in my lap. "Excuse me. What did you just say?"

All eyes locked on Elles. "Nothing. I said she's alone."

"No. The other part. The pregnant one."

"Oh, that. I don't know. I wasn't really thinking when I said it."

Frustration boiled very near the surface. "Elyse. I like you very much, but if you don't quit your yammering, I cannae be responsible for what happens next."

"I don't know if she's pregnant. She's late. That's all. She's late. I went over yesterday, and I brought some wine. She wouldn't drink it. So then I started giving her a hard time, and she mentioned she was late."

"She didn't think this was important news to share with her husband?"

"What news? There's no news ."

"I have to go."

Trick clapped me on the back again, damn near rattling my teeth. "Go get her."

Pregnant or not, we needed to have a conversation. I had a lot I needed to clear up with her, starting with this revelation. Pulling out my phone, I sent her a quick text message.

Me: I know I'm the last person you want to talk to right now, but that's too damn bad. I'm coming home. Stay right where you are. We need to have a conversation.

She didn't answer, and that sent a jolt of fear through me, but it didn't stop me. I had let fear get in my way more times than I could count, and it wasn't happening again.

Two hours later, after one missed ferry and some stop-and-go traffic on the way to the terminal, I finally pulled into the driveway. Lights were on in the house, her car was in the driveway, and my stupid heart was pounding. The thought that she might be pregnant wasn't even the most important thing. That would be happy news. It would be one of the greatest things that could have happened to us. But add that to the notion that she wasn't talking to me, and I was an absolute disaster.

I came in like a damn wrecking ball, swinging hard, ready to prove my worth and show her I'd be the best damn father there was if we were gonna be parents. And if we weren't . . . I had plenty of other things to prove to her. Starting with exactly how much I loved her.

BECCA

I stepped out of the bath, my skin hot and pink from the too-hot water and the length of time I spent soaking. It had been too long, but I didn't know how to face the rest of the day. Sure, I was hurt by what happened with Taylor, hurt that he must've told his sister in much greater detail than I'd shared about our bargain, even after everything that had happened between us. But even more than that, I was upset with myself for not being able to just let it go. It wouldn't have been hard. All I needed to do was tell him I understood and move on. Except adding on the articles, his comments to the press, and the divorce . . . I wasn't going to stay in a relationship that made me feel so worthless.

So I'd stuck to my guns and made us both miserable. But the worst part was he let me. He didn't even try to fight for us.

I stared at myself in the mirror. Eyes that were once bright were now dull and lifeless. With a sigh, I applied my skincare routine, knowing it wouldn't do me any good to wallow and neglect my self-care. Then I wrapped up in a towel and grabbed my half-empty wineglass from the small table Taylor had gotten me to put beside my bathtub. I could hear his voice clear in my head.

'You shouldn't have to balance your wine precariously on the side of the tub, hen. Let me do this for

you.' Of course, that memory brought a fresh wave of tears because I missed him so much. All I wanted was for us to reconcile. For us to be together again. I didn't need anything else. Just him. That was it. We'd figure out the rest. We had to.

Wiping away the tears, I padded out of the bath and to the bedroom, then put on a pair of fresh underwear and, because I was a disaster, I pulled his jersey over my head. I inhaled deeply, taking in his scent. It was already fading. What would I do when it didn't smell like him anymore? When he got traded and left me and found something infinitely better. Because there was no doubt in my mind that he would.

I took my phone off the charger and made an effort not to immediately check my messages, but when I did, my heart fluttered because I saw his name.

Hook: I know I'm the last person you want to talk to right now, but that's too damn bad. I'm coming home. Stay right where you are. We need to have a conversation.

I should've been hesitant, worried even, but I needed him more than I wanted to be upset. He was coming for me. He wanted me, and I was so damn happy about it. Pulling my hair into a messy wet bun, I raced downstairs to meet him. It had been two hours since he sent that message.

My heart stopped when I saw him on the

porch, his hands braced on his knees as he sat on the steps. Instead of pulling open the door and throwing myself at him, I forced myself to stay calm as I walked to the kitchen and poured us each a glass of wine. I took a fortifying gulp and then made my way to the porch.

I opened the door and sat next to him, handing him a glass of wine.

"Lass, I don't know what to say."

"It's not you that has to say anything. I overreacted. I'm sorry."

"No, you didn't. I should have come to your defense. Immediately. I shouldn't have mentioned a single word about our arrangement to my sister."

"Why not? I told mine. I'd be an incredible hypocrite if I was angry with you for sharing something so important about your life with someone you love and trust. Sure, she shouldn't have told anyone, but she was just trying to protect her brother. I understand that. I've gone to bat for my sister more than once, and I would do it again and again."

"I sure as hell should've told you what I was doing with that lawyer. He was helping me with contract things. He's my friend. You have to know how much I love you. I'd never leave you, Tink. You're mine. Forever." God, the way his voice broke as he tried to get through those words.

My lower lip quivered. "I do. I'm sorry I shouldn't have doubted you, but that article . . ."

"They've already taken it down. It might have started as truth, but it didn't stay that way. And no one gets to say anything like that about you. You're mine, and I couldn't be prouder to call you my wife."

Here I went again, crying. I took a deep breath to steady myself and then lifted my glass to my lips, but he batted it out of my hand, red wine splashing across the cement as the glass shattered.

"What the hell, Taylor?"

"What in God's name are you doing? Ye cannae be drinking in your condition, hen."

"What do you mean? Yes, I can."

"Not when you're . . ." All the wind left his sails as his brow furrowed.

"What? Not when I'm what, Taylor?"

"Listen, don't get mad at Elles. But she told me . . ."

"What did she tell you?"

"That you were . . . you know . . ."

"Oh my God. Did that bitch tell you I was pregnant?"

"Ye dinnae think I deserved to know?"

"No, Taylor. I didn't think you deserved to know because it's not true."

"Hen, she said you told her you were late."

"Yes. I was a couple days late because I was stressed out."

"How do you know it's because you're stressed? What if you're late because—"

"Taylor, I'm on birth control, and if you must know, my period started yesterday. Right after she left."

All his bravado vanished, and he looked at me, embarrassment clear on his face.

"I'm sorry. I overreacted."

I chuckled. "You think? Do you really think I would not tell you if I thought I was pregnant?"

"Aye. Not right now. I wouldn't deserve to know."

"Yes, you would. Why would you say that?"

"Is that something you're ready for now? Kids?"

"Yeah, I want everything with you. Even if it means I have to start baking and manage the business remotely when you get traded, if that happens."

"I'm not going to be traded."

"Really? But it's still a possibility, right? I mean, we'd be stupid to think it wasn't?"

"No, I'm not going to be, because depending on what the doctor says, this season might be my last with the Cyclones. If not, I'll give it one more with the NHL. Then I'm retiring."

"You're not doing this for me, are you? Taylor,

I'll never forgive myself if you give up your whole life's dream because of me."

"No. I'm not doing it because of you. I'm doing it because I need to. My knee is shot. It's a disaster. I need to let it rest, and that includes not playing hockey. I talked to my agent on my way here, and there's an assistant coaching position open that will allow me to stay on with the Cyclones after my contract is up. All I have to do is accept the offer."

"There is? That's amazing."

"Yeah, it really is. Apparently, Maverick has been trying to talk to me about it for weeks, but . . ."

"You wouldn't answer your phone."

"Exactly."

"So," I started, leaning into his side. "What are you going to say?"

"My favorite word. The best thing you've ever said to me, in fact."

"What is that?"

I smiled as he wrapped his arm around me and pressed his lips to my ear.

"Yes."

EPILOGUE

BECCA

Hook: Are you ever gonna come back from the bakery, lass? Or do I have to come in there and get you?

Me: What are you talking about? I've been in the bathtub for the last fifteen minutes.

I watched the little response bubbles bounce around on the screen, but Taylor didn't reply. Instead, not two minutes later, a soft knock on the bathroom door had me pulling the bubbles up to cover my breasts.

"Can I come in?" he asked, an adorable hesitance in his voice.

I giggled. "Of course you can come in. You've never asked before."

"Well, it just seems different now."

"Why?"

"Because before, I was trying to get a rise out of you, but now I want you to want me."

"Taylor, of course I want you, and while I appreciate you being a gentleman and respecting my privacy, you have literally touched and kissed every inch of my body. There's nothing in here you haven't seen."

I let my gaze travel over his bare tattooed chest and down to the crotch of his... damn, his gray sweatpants, which were already tented at the mention of what his lips did to me just this morning.

"Do you want to join me? There's room in here for two, even if you are a big burly Scot."

"I wish I could, more than anything, actually. But I have to leave in about thirty minutes."

"Oh, why?"

"I'm having a meeting with Maverick and the coaching staff."

"Are they officially announcing your retirement?"

"They are. I had a call from my doctor, and my knee's not even good for another season. Now's the time to step down. If they can find me a place now, I want to stay here in Seattle with you. I love it here. It reminds me of home, and the most important thing is you're here and you're mine. I don't want to be parted from you."

Without giving him any warning, I stood and stepped out of the tub, naked and wet, covered in bubbles. Then I wrapped my arms around him and kissed him long and deep.

"Lass, I need to get ready."

"It won't take long. Come on, Taylor, let's put those limber hip flexors of yours to good use."

His tongue explored my mouth, all fire and passion and hunger. I should have cared that I hadn't taken my birth control. I should have warned him we were being reckless, but he was staying for us, and we were a family.

He walked me back to the bed and laid me on the mattress. The way he stood over me, staring down at my naked body, at every curve, every inch, had me so wet and ready. Open for him.

"Fuck, lass, you're glistening for me. How can I go without a taste?"

I glanced at the clock. "You have five minutes to make me come and another five to make yourself come, and if you're lucky, maybe you'll knock me up while you're at it."

He snagged a pillow and placed it on the floor before he got down on his knees, careful of his healing injury. Both hands splayed on my inner thighs, he spread me wide, and those beautiful eyes of his locked on mine from across my body.

"What did you just say?"

"I said, maybe if you're lucky, you'll knock me up. My birth control ran out, and I haven't been able to get new pills yet."

"So I either pull out, or we start trying for a baby? Are you really ready?"

"Are you?"

"I want everything with you, Becca. I want as many kids as you want to give me. Anything I make with you in this life is a gift as long as that's what you want."

"I'm ready, Taylor."

And I was. I could picture him taking our kids out to skate at the rink, teaching them how to play hockey. Protecting them. Loving them. Worshiping the family we made. After seeing him with his family in Scotland, I knew there was nothing he was more suited for. It was the thing he had been missing here in the States, but I could help with that. And I would.

Before I could say another word, his mouth was on me, sucking, teasing, tasting, and biting. His fingers followed and then worked in a rhythm with his tongue. Inside and around, over and over, until my thighs were quaking. I clenched my fingers in his hair as I came with a ragged moan on the bed, reaching a climax in less than five minutes.

"Thank you very much."

He backed away, wiping the back of his hand over his lips before he freed himself from his sweats, gripped me under the hips, and shoved me farther back onto the bed.

Then he positioned himself between my legs,

notching his cock at my entrance, spreading his thighs wide, just like I'd seen him do countless times as he stretched on the ice.

"Are you ready?"

"I'm so ready. Fill me up, Taylor."

He rolled his hips forward and sank deep in one long thrust, and I cried out and clenched around him. The way he had to grit his teeth and close his eyes as he stilled himself to take control did things to me.

"Don't do that if you want me to last."

"I don't want you to last. You have three minutes left, and then you have to go. And you can't go see my brother-in-law smelling of my pussy."

"If you think I'm washing you off me, you are very wrong, Mrs. Savage."

I loved the idea that he would go around all day smelling me on him. Tasting me. He rolled his hips slowly, hitting every nerve ending on the way in and then out, and it wasn't long before both of us were panting, close to reaching our climaxes. I dug my nails into his back and dragged him down to me so he could kiss me. As he came with a quiet, shuddering gasp of pleasure, I followed.

"I love you, Taylor. Scottish bad boy of hockey or not, you're mine, and this arrangement we made was the greatest decision of my life."

He held himself up on his elbows before

pressing a kiss to my nose. "Who would have thought the pirate would have ended up with the pixie in the end?"

"I don't think you're a pirate anymore."

"Oh, no?"

"No."

"What am I, then?"

"One-hundred percent mine."

"Damn right."

SNEAK PEEK: THE VIRGIN PROPOSAL

TRICK

"I HAVE A PROPOSITION FOR YOU," I muttered, shaking my head as I stared down at the Meet-Cupid app on my phone. "What the hell is wrong with you?"

The cool night air coming off the water served to sober me up a little as the party inside Big Deck's house went on. I was such an idiot. I had zero game. I might be a star hockey player, but that was all I had going for me. I could skate and shoot. But scoring with the fairer sex? Forget it.

The only reason I agreed to be on this dating app was to help me find someone since talking to women seemed to cause nausea inducing panic that had me internally curled up in a ball of insecurity. I was tired of being alone. Tired of being the focused athlete who didn't have anyone to share my life with. Did I think I was going to find the woman I'd marry on Meet-Cupid? No. But dipping my toe into dating with the app when I was hopeless on my own was the only way I'd ever get over my awkwardness.

The contract wasn't so bad either. I liked the extra money. Not gonna lie.

I stared down at the message I'd stupidly sent to the girl I'd matched with, @TheScarlettSiren.

@HaTrick: I have a proposition for you.

Of course, she didn't answer. She hadn't been online yet. Not that we'd spoken. I woke up with a notification that we'd matched and she hadn't declined after I swiped up on her as someone I was interested in. Honestly, I hadn't even looked at her photo after reading about her. Twenty-five, a baker, owns her own business, loves dogs and cake. She sounded like my perfect woman.

I tipped my water to my lips and took a long swallow as the stars shimmered in the velvet black sky overhead. The moon was a heavy glimmering weight reflecting over the water. Fuck, it was pretty out here. Of all the places I'd lived, Washington might have been my favorite.

The glissando of a harp—yes, I knew what that was, my mother was a professional harpist, give me a break—filled the air as a notification came through from my phone.

"What the hell was that?" I asked no one.

I glanced down at the screen and my heart gave a little stutter. A notification from Meet-Cupid.

@TheScarlettSiren is within one mile of your location. Send a message?

Oh fuck. What should I do?

"Be cool, Trick. Be fucking cool. Don't propose marriage the first time you see her. Don't tell her you're a virgin who doesn't know how to talk to girls. Jesus, don't call her a girl. She's a woman. You're a man."

The back door slid open and Elles walked out with the sister-in-law of the team owner. I couldn't remember her name, but she was really damn pretty. They were all the way at the end of the deck, laughing together, the wind blowing her blond locks behind her.

She pulled her phone from her pocket and smiled down at it before she began typing.

A moment later, my phone chimed again, loudly. She looked at me with shock on her face before smiling.

@TheScarlettSiren: A proposition? Tell me more.

Contemporary Romance

<u>Until the Stars Fade</u> **Get this FREE by joining my Facebook Group: Loraine Lovers**

Anything For Love

The Baby Proposition

The Dating Playbook

The Marriage Arrangement

The Virgin Proposal

Wilde Horse Ranch

Wild Ride (Accidental Marriage)

Wild Mistake (Best friend's little sister)

An Irresistible Chance (Single dad)

Drive Me Wild (M/M enemies to lovers)

Ryker Ranch

Saddle Up (Opposites Attract)

Bucked Off (Fake Fiancee)

Ridden Hard (Surprise Baby)

Roped Tight (Second Chance M/M)

Reined In

KB Worlds Everyday Heroes/Ryker Ranch

Ignite (Age-Gap/Forbidden Romance)

The Royal Virgins

The Virgin's Playboy Prince

The Virgin's Royal Guard

The Virgin's Forbidden Lord

The Virgin's Fake Fiancé

The Cocktail Girls

His Whiskey Sour (A Stand Alone Rock Star Romance)

ABOUT THE AUTHOR

Kim writes steamy contemporary and sexy paranormal romance. **You'll find her paranormal romances written under the name K. Loraine and her contemporaries as Kim Loraine.** Don't worry, you'll get the same level of swoon-worthy heroes, sassy heroines, and an eventual HEA.

When not writing, she's busy herding cats (raising kids), trying to keep her house sort of clean, and dreaming up ways for fictional couples to meet.

Sign up to get updates on all of Kim's new releases

Be sure to follow me on Bookbub!

Join my Facebook reader group and get a free book!

www.facebook.com/groups/kimlorainebooks

KIM LORAINE
ROMANCE AUTHOR

- facebook.com/kimlorainewriter
- twitter.com/kimloraine2
- instagram.com/kimloraineauthor
- bookbub.com/authors/kim-loraine
- amazon.com/author/kimloraine
- goodreads.com/kimloraine

CPSIA information can be obtained
at www.ICGtesting.com
Printed in the USA
BVHW070132121122
651754BV00008B/266

9 781088 061282